KISS THE RAKE HELLO

TRACY SUMNER

Kiss the Rake Hello

Copyright © 2023 by Tracy Sumner

Editor: Elizabeth J. Connor

The Marginatrix

Cover designer: Mandy Koehler Designs

All rights reserved.

No part of this book may be reproduced in any form or by any electronic or mechanical means, including information storage and retrieval systems, without written permission from the author, except for the use of brief quotations in a book review.

Nothing ever becomes real till it is experienced.
~John Keats

The Troublesome Trio
Cortland

CHAPTER 1

WHERE A SECOND CHANCE PRESENTS ITSELF

Hampstead, England 1816

*T*he flutter of awareness caught her like a needle beneath the skin.

Alexandra shaded her eyes, searching the broad bands of sunlight scattered across the stable yard. A spark skated across her skin, similar to the shock when her slipper chafed a woolen carpet. The man who'd laughed and caught her attention looked familiar, something about him seizing her breath in an uncommon way.

Uncommon because the woman the *ton* called the Wintry Widow rarely experienced jolts of any kind.

The male curiosity was sitting in the flatbed of a workman's cart, long legs swinging, his left bootheel tapping the rimmed metal frame and flexing his hip in an appealing way. As the sun shifted behind a cloud and he came into view, she realized his display was more of a sprawl.

And his looks were as stellar as the display.

Hair the color of ripe chestnuts, too long for fashion, dusted a marble sculpture of a jaw. The strands were curling slightly in the post-drizzle air, an enticement she didn't want to appreciate but couldn't help noticing. Reflecting the casual setting, he was dressed informally. Scuffed boots she would nevertheless wager were Hoby-crafted, his fine trousers sporting a tear in one knee as if he'd gone down hard but not cared enough to repair the damage. A cravat looped carelessly about his neck, the dangling ends leading her gaze to the undone button of his waistcoat.

The *bottom* button.

From there, a mere drop of her gaze, and she was confronted with a set of muscular thighs and everything wondrous resting in between.

Her visual quest taking her places it hadn't in years. Places it shouldn't.

As the unwelcome rush of attraction cascaded through her, Alexandra shoved to her feet, stumbling into the workbench at her side. The filly next to her whinnied and sidestepped in alarm.

"Hold up, Mountbatten, or you'll have me tools strewn in the soil and this young beast kicking out at us."

Alexandra laughed, hoping false delight had the power to hide her bewildering reaction. "There was a bee, and you know I hate them." Waving the rag she held before her scorching cheeks, she shrugged weakly. "And I'm no longer a Mountbatten. It's Lady Amberly now."

"Lass, you'll always be a Mountbatten." Seamus Doherty scrubbed his knuckles across his leather apron and rose on creaking knees, his expression more than a touch knowing. His eyes glowed the color of burnt timber in a face defeated by time and exposure. "That incident with the bee has to be going on twenty years past though I easily bring it to mind. Your teensy arm swelled to the size of a ham hock. Mrs. Dansen had me fashion a poultice. Same as I make for equine ailments, dog turd and beetles."

She grimaced. His miracle salve had worked, but she'd smelled ripe for a week—and her terror of bees had been born.

"Your parents were away in Scotland, I think it was." Seamus ran his hand down the mount's glistening coat. "Or maybe Wales."

Alexandra pressed her hand to her belly, surprised at the flurry of emotion that hit her when she recalled her parents, a couple who'd been *away* for most of her childhood. Away for good when a carriage accident removed them from this world when she was twelve. Seamus and his family, her father's farrier since he rose from the position of lead groom the month before she was born, and Mrs. Dansen, her housekeeper, had raised her after that. A series of governesses and companions allowing her to reside in her childhood home, Hampton Court, until her marriage. Consumption had taken Mrs. Dansen, and an unlucky tumble from his mount on a hillside course in Brittany had claimed Alexandra's husband of five years, Viscount Amberly, last winter.

For a multitude of reasons, it was hard to mourn him.

With as little direction as rubbish wafting about in a stormy gust, she'd left Amberly's estate in Hertfordshire to return to Hampton Court, an unentailed property miraculously hers and hers alone. A former merchant's manor, it was modestly dilapidated, reportedly haunted, and thoroughly beloved. She'd merely wanted to live out her days here, in peace. However, due to a lackluster Season, society's regard had followed her, the scandal sheets mentioning her more than she cared for. Would the Wintry Widow marry again? Take a lover? Retire to the country to never return? The only benefit to her union with Amberly had been the ability to fade like fog in sunlight. Just another married chit in the *ton*.

When she'd once wanted, well, *things*.

She rolled her fingers into a fist, her surge of temper easily squelched. Rebellion at this stage would get her nowhere. And who in heaven's name would she rebel with?

Unable to check herself, Alexandra shot a side-glance at the stranger lounging on the cart. He looked like a man able to answer philosophical questions.

Her pensioning agreement with Seamus had allowed him to outfit the small shed behind the stable as an office, where he welcomed business from the village and beyond. His son and grandson had joined him in the enterprise and gents routinely traveled from London for his expert knowledge of horses. It was difficult to find someone who could properly shoe a horse.

She delayed as long as she could before asking, "The man over there, is he one of your clients?"

Seamus tightened the filly's bridle, his smile blooming in a way that meant his delight was going to pinch. "He is, indeed. Got a shoddy shoeing last week in a stall near Hyde Park. Left this beauty limping like she had a stone wedged in her hoof. They don't teach the smithing profession as they used to. I can't even find lads willing to apprentice. Could double me business if I could." Seamus squinted at her across the sleek rise of the horse's neck. "If it weren't a catastrophe for a gel to be in trade, guaranteed expulsion from society, you'd be the chief soul I'd enter into agreement with. Except for me, you know more about this than anyone in England."

Regrettably, this was true.

Since the age of ten, Alexandra had covertly trained under Seamus as industriously as his son, an improper proficiency for the daughter of an earl. A recently widowed viscountess. A *woman*. She'd had to pretend ignorance about so many issues—history, politics, art—that it had become second nature. As the *ton* liked nothing better than silly fools.

Again, she glanced across the courtyard. "He looks bored. Ready to scurry back to Town as soon as his mount is able to carry him."

The lazy smile, the rumpled coat, the ripped breeches. That deliciously dawdling length of silk trailing down his chest, leading her attention into murky waters. No man in the village looked like this. She'd have remembered. Perhaps used the attractive vision to her benefit on a lonely night. Satisfaction came by her own hand.

It was certain her husband had never brought her pleasure.

If the stranger on Seamus' cart felt the weight of her gaze, he ignored it, ignored *her*, speaking to the groom with a half-grin splitting his cheeks, long legs still swinging. Confidence in repose. Leaning back, he muscled a flask from the inside pocket of his coat and lifted it to his lips. Alexandra watched in captivated horror as his throat pulled as he swallowed, his cheeks hollowing.

A burst of internal sunlight hit her, making her skin glow, the

4

sensation claiming her body irrefutable. She recognized lust, even if she'd had little exposure.

As if he felt it, too, his gaze touched her, his lips tightening for an instant before a shadowy smile settled back into place, and he turned away.

Alexandra scowled and wrapped the rag around her fist. Even as she'd prayed for invisibility for much of her life, she wasn't used to being overlooked. Her keen attractiveness, bequeathed from her mother, was a curse that had rendered her first Season her *only*. She'd had offers, more than any sensible young woman could refuse without guidance—and she'd not been sensible or had guidance. Rather, she'd been desperate to escape the chaos. Roses filling the foyer, calling cards spilling from silver salvers. Moonlit near-kisses, groping hands and drunken leers.

One gentleman—Baron Neeley?—had stood beneath her bedchamber window and sung ballads until her servants hustled him down the mews. The gossip rags had detailed the exploit the following morning as London's breath caught in wait for the next scandal. Feverish and troubled, she'd accepted Amberly's offer on the first asking. Because he'd seemed to understand. He'd seemed to want more than a beautiful trinket dangling from his pocket like a fob. He'd seemed to want *her*. Promised to give her the family she'd never had.

When he'd merely wished to possess her dowry. She'd no idea the enormous gambling debts he'd incurred the year before their marriage.

Seamus gave the filly another gentle stroke, preparing to lead him across the courtyard to his owner. "You don't recognize him, then?"

Oh. "Should I?"

Seamus ticked his chin toward the cart. "He's one of the DeWitt trio. Twins and another so close in age you'd think he come spilling out with the other two. Lads always brawling on the front lawn, ruining gardens and breaking windows. You must recollect. Now breaking hearts, if you believe the chatter. Grown men's antics. I had to get after them more times than I care to recall. But boys will be boys, won't they? I should know as I have two of me own rough-housers."

The rag slipped from Alexandra's fingers to the dirt. "The Duke of Herschel."

Separated by more years than could sustain a friendship, especially between the sexes, the neighboring DeWitt boys had been a thorn in her side. Teasing pranks. Games she'd not wanted to play but been forced into. Their bows and arrows scattered across the lawn. Lads growing into men, never to be seen again when they were feasibly becoming interesting. She entered her first season while they headed to Eton or Harrow or Rugby. She'd been living alone by then with a string of inattentive governesses and jaded companions, pondering an uncertain future. She'd not thought of the DeWitts in ages.

Seamus started his trek across the yard, the glance he tossed over his shoulder highly amused. "No, lass, the other one. The second son. The true rabblerouser."

Alexandra's breath seized. *Cortland*. The specimen of masculine perfection lounging across the way was the mature version of her childhood tormentor? She searched her memory. Chestnut curls and a gaze as green as Christmas holly. Gangly, his arms too long for his body, his smile gap-toothed and teeming with mischief. He'd been behind her every time she turned around an eternity ago. Underfoot, an annoyance, a nuisance. The younger twin by mere minutes she recalled, either safeguarding him from the burden of a title or snatching it from his grasp.

She would love to know which he believed it was.

He'd tried to kiss her once, a charmingly awkward production in the kitchen garden. He couldn't have been more than fourteen to her near nineteen.

As she stared, the world narrowed until she viewed it through a scope. The stunning creature shoving off the donkey cart to claim his horse, hooking his boot in the stirrup and pulling his broad body astride it was little Cort DeWitt? Why, the top of his head had barely reached Alexandra's chin during that kiss, the difference in height part of the reason for its inelegance.

Although she avoided the scandals sheets unless forced to read them, she'd nonetheless heard about his antics. The Troublesome Trio, the *ton* called the DeWitt brothers. A moniker almost as silly as the Wintry Widow.

Sighing, Alexandra blinked the mist of the past from her eyes.

The allegations about his outrageous liaisons now made sense. Life was easy for brothers of dukes who looked like gods.

Bewildered, she crouched to retrieve the rag, the sound of hoof-beats meaning she wouldn't have to spend another second trying to unravel the incredible mystery of passing time.

Cort was out of sorts.

Off-kilter. Riding a fine edge of irritability.

He knew it and so did the cluster of dimwits in the Hanover Square ballroom.

They stayed away, eyeing him with wary vigilance from his position tucked in a dark corner. In the shadows, not where he usually kept himself. Just beyond, dancers circled the floor in time to the muffled strains from the orchestra on the balcony above, diaphanous silk and satin coloring a kingdom of gray. Chalk dust scattered on slick marble to keep people from slipping to their bums stung his nose and made him wish for an unpolluted breath.

Rolling his shoulders inside his superfine coat, he sighed, realizing how detached he was from this world. The enticements—music, drink, *women*—held no value at present. Not when he'd left part of his mind in a Hampstead stable courtyard, with a woman he'd not anticipated seeing again in this lifetime.

And if he'd halfheartedly imagined seeing her, he'd hoped his reaction would be different.

As it was, his heart had taken the predictable leap from his chest and landed somewhere in the vicinity of her muddy boots. Like they stood in that garden with him bouncing on his toes to reach her lips.

Beautiful Alexandra Mountbatten, the feisty chit who'd loved rejecting him.

Fuck.

His boyhood bane, his childish infatuation, sharing the same breathing space for the first time in years. She'd looked different—yet not. Much to his dismay, he'd recognized her the instant he walked into the courtyard, cursing his brother for his misinformation that she no longer resided in Hampstead. Still circling the horses, her passion even back then, a mature rendering of the carefree girl he'd cherished. Her gown a brutal jest on fashion, her cheeks unsuitably sun-kissed, her hair a heavy, mahogany tangle atop her head.

He polished his hand across his chin, his breath quickening. *Ah,* he remembered that hair. The kind that made a man imagine wrapping it around his fist and tugging as he slid inside her. Gently but with purpose, until time dissolved like mist on the sea.

Her lips, regretfully, had been the exact ones from his memory, the most gorgeous mouth of any woman he'd met to this day. Pink and pouting when she'd looked at him back in the day, the bottom rolling over the top.

God, her sulks had sent him into an adolescent frenzy.

Throughout his childhood, she'd done her best, a notable job, actually, of ignoring the bloody hell out of him. When all he'd wanted was a word. A glance. A kiss. When she'd been his senior by enough years to count. Too many, he supposed, in fairness. Maturing into a woman while he'd been waiting for fur to sprout on his bollocks.

His brothers had often told him to pick on someone his own age.

At some point, he had.

Memories buffeted him despite his best effort to chuck them from his mind, proving he shouldn't have consumed the second glass of champagne. The way she'd held her head at a slight angle when she was thinking. Her supremely agile seat atop a horse. Her smile, buttery soft for those held in her affection. Her laugh, deep but with a supple edge. He'd been attracted not only to her beauty, but also her wit, her intelligence.

Empathy had come later, when he'd observed her watching his

family interact with her heart in her eyes. That bit drawing him in when he'd hardly known what he was about.

A mingled image tore through Cort. The girl from the past and the woman in the courtyard, her lush body sprawled beneath his, her lips parting, her words welcoming this time. Attraction tolled like a bell, a rusty, neglected emotion. He didn't want to find this vision of her appealing when it held no chance of fulfillment. Not now, when he knew better.

About everything.

He was changed since Waterloo, the final scrap of innocence sliced away on a blood-stained battlefield. Though he was trying mightily to guide his boat into calmer waters and relieve his family and friends of the burden of unease. The sons and brothers returning from battle were cause for concern, as they had a blank emptiness behind their eyes they couldn't hide, solve for, or remedy. He attended every function he was invited to, was an able brother to a duke, when he'd rather be in his set of rooms at the Albany working on his engine designs. A hobby society thought peculiar for a three-minutes-away-from-being-a-duke bloke.

When the simple truth was, Cort no longer belonged.

And there was only so much he was willing to do to pretend he did.

"If you don't erase that scowl from your face, you're going to forever wreck your charming reputation. Countess Rashford is waiting for you to make a move. She's been watching us all night. If you're the gentleman she's chosen this month, consider yourself fortunate and ask her to dance." As he was inclined to do, Cort's twin, Knoxville, the Duke of Herschel, gave him a shove that knocked him out of the shadows and into the band of candlelight cast from the chandelier.

Stumbling into a footman's path, Cort deftly snatched two flutes from a tray and forced one into his brother's hand.

Taking a lingering sip, Knox hummed, a sign of forthcoming wisdom. "The countess is a tigress in bed, or so they say. Maybe a torrid affair could be the thing to pull you back. You would have jumped on this opportunity, quite literally, before. You're getting too used to the ease of paid explorations when lightskirts should be reserved for desperate phases only."

A tigress, Cort thought dispassionately, although he kept his indifference to himself. No man would admit, even to his brother, the weariness accompanying such a fantasy. It was true that courtesans were his current yet infrequent stratagem. He'd tried slipping back into society in a normal roguish manner upon his return—bored wives, ravenous widows—but he'd found he was no longer able to play the game competently enough to survive it.

If he'd been a wolf, he wasn't one anymore. And marriage wasn't a commitment he could imagine himself making in such uncertain times. "Pull me back from what?"

Knox's fingers tightened around the flute's stem hard enough to shatter crystal.

"I had to do something," Cort whispered, telling himself it would be the last time they had this conversation. When it came up often. Too often. "Second sons mean little in our world, Knox. You know this. Cambridge wasn't taking me back after the unpleasantness, although I honestly didn't know the materials were combustible. I apologized profusely even as I was beating out the flames consuming my waistcoat. My belly was charred for weeks. It was a prank that went awry, and I wasn't going to Father again. Not this time. He paid for the mirror in Eleby's ballroom, you recall, when his daughter threw the vase at me. So I bought the commission with my own funds and sent back what I could until I paid for the damage."

The rest he'd compensated for in ways money couldn't buy.

"Second sons of dukes don't go to *war*, Cort. They blow up university labs and are gently castigated for their transgressions. Then they return to a life of dissipation and delight." He tossed back his champagne, laughing when he wasn't amused. "I rather preferred your infamy for mischief. The boat you capsized on the Thames. The time you spent two days lost in the woods in Hampstead when we were boys. That calamity with the henhouse you erected that one summer. This soldiering mess..." He shrugged, running out of steam like a kettle taken off a burner. "I can't grasp your decision, even now. It keeps me up at night envisioning it."

Cort rubbed the back of his neck, which had suddenly gone hot. Regarding those poor chickens, he'd not realized foxes could tear through wire so easily. He'd cried when he'd seen the destruction. "I was good at it," he explained when he didn't need to explain a damned thing.

"At killing?"

Cort turned on his brother, as always, experiencing a jolt at seeing himself reflected back. They looked so much alike that they'd taken classes for each other at Eton with teachers none the wiser. Heeding rumors, upon entry to Cambridge, the administrators had forced them to attend classes together. When anyone who knew them understood Cort had Knox by a solid two inches in height. "At *leading*. I never had a chance to do that before. Dissipation doesn't suit. I'm too restless to allow it."

Knox's shoulders slumped. "If I ever made you feel—"

"You didn't. I don't wish for a dukedom any more than you did. I merely had to grow up." The memory of cannon fire rippled over him, along with the scent of gunpowder and the stinging odor of scorched earth. But he could live with those things, *his* life. "For all the event changed me, I did. Grow up. Allow me this in the manner in which I chose to do it. I certainly gave you the same opportunity."

Knox fell silent, rubbing the rim of his flute over his lips.

Cort waited, understanding his brother's need to work through a problem one cautious step at a time. They were vastly different in this way as Cort made decisions seconds *after* committing. A problem, according to his family. However, he was being honest with the one person he loved most in the world. He didn't want the title. In fact, he'd thanked the heavens more times than he could count for arriving second. Those three minutes had given him freedom. Liberty that at one time had confounded him with its vastness but now seemed divine intervention.

Knox rocked back on his heels with a sigh. "I'd ask a favor of you, if I could. Parliament is in session for another month, and my time is limited. Damien is off working on some mysterious project, and I can't ask him."

Cort exhaled softly, staring at the bubbles riding his champagne. He knew this was the launch of a request he'd want to reject. Knox only brought up his duties in the House of Lords if he wished to guilt Cort into easy acceptance. "I'm scared to ask, but what?"

"I know you were out there earlier today, but I've scheduled repairs in Hampstead that need supervision. The north section of the roof, the scullery floor. You could work on your designs. It should take a week or so, at most. The village has enough entertainments to keep you busy. A willing widow or two that I recall." He flicked his hand, his flute glittering in the candlelight. "You always loved it there more than anyone."

Cort tossed back his drink, champagne hitting his brain in a rush and bringing a murky haze to his vision. Something about this request felt like foreshadowing when he wasn't a man who believed in inevitability.

Knox saluted a passing group with his glass. "She doesn't live there anymore. Moved away when she married, though Hampton Court is still in the family. Unentailed, if you can believe it."

Cort made the pointless effort, a two-second action, to argue. Or laugh. Then he stopped himself with a whispered curse instead. Everyone had known about his fixation with Alexandra Mountbatten from the time he was ten years old. *Except* Alexandra Mountbatten. Why debate a moot bit of utterly substantiated history? "Amberly. She moved away when she married Viscount Amberly." A few weeks, give or take, before he'd destroyed the Cambridge lab. He'd often questioned if the news of his neighbor's betrothal to a reprobate of the first order had lit a reckless fire beneath him.

His fuse never took much to get it burning.

For weeks after, he hadn't been able to get it—*her*—out of his mind. By that time, his dreams had been filled with lewd illustrations, each one bearing her likeness. Uncreative, perhaps, but her gorgeous lips wrapped around his cock had been the most prominent.

Not a boy's cravings, these.

"It's been ages since I last saw her. Sometime before we left for school," Cort lied, glancing around for a footman. That damned kiss had occurred on a break from Eton. If they were going to discuss childhood obsessions, Cort needed another drink. A stronger one. Two, in fact. Or six. "Old news, Your Grace. I'm past that. A thousand tups past."

His brother grinned and knocked him in the shoulder again, sending him skipping to the side. He hated it when Knox did that. "So you'll do it? Go to Hampstead and supervise the repairs?"

If he closed his eyes, Cort could see the fields behind the stately manor they'd spent summers in while growing up, a gilded landscape racing to the horizon. Full vistas and star-lit skies. The air scented with grass or hay or hydrangea. The home had been his mother's, a place of refuge and pleasure. She'd passed there, as had his father. Skinned knees and grimy feet, swimming in the lake behind the house, archery in the triangle of woodland between the estate and the postal road. Hampstead wasn't far, a two-hour ride from London, but it'd been far enough as a lad to seem another world. Full of dreams and adventure.

Knox was right about one thing. Cort's heart had always been in Hampstead.

Restless, he signaled a footman, needing liquid courage more than ever. "I'll go. I'm due to show designs to McKinley in a month, so I can use the week in Hampstead to finalize my drawings." Cort had a plan, a damn good one, to make his fortune through the invention of a high-pressure cylinder for steam engines, which was, he believed, the future of transportation. Engines that could take more of a beating were the only way to bring prices down and steer the industry away from its reliance on cheap, filthy coal. He had a mind for mechanics; there wasn't a device he couldn't take apart and put back together in minutes. The quietude of his work matched his amended personality, if it *was* changed, perfectly.

As did his fierce need to make his own way, a truth his twin didn't understand as his path had been laid out for him since birth.

Three minutes that had drawn clear lines between them.

But Hampstead felt like a risky roll of the dice.

Because Cort still remembered the first time he'd seen Alexandra Mountbatten, now Alexandra Mountbatten Rashing, the widowed Viscountess Amberly. A girl he'd once called Alex. A tattered gown an inch too short batting her trim ankles, a wrinkled cap shoved on her head, her luscious hair a tangle beneath it. An earl's daughter with dirt on her chin and ragged fingernails, a smile she unleashed without reservation, nothing like the guarded darlings in Mayfair. She'd fairly glowed with vigor, and he'd never forget the punch to his gut each time he'd seen her.

Not dissimilar from the sensation today when he'd realized who was helping Seamus shoe his mount.

Maybe he'd idolized her because she'd looked through him, over him, *past* him. Sons of dukes, even second sons, weren't used to being disregarded. This afternoon, however, in a deserted stable courtyard, he'd felt the weight of awareness circling, a woman's gaze hot upon him. A buzz he recognized.

Thankfully, he wasn't that scrawny lad anymore.

After years of silent worship, he was due some luck with this chit, wasn't he? If she were the one to pine, should they chance to meet again, that wouldn't be the worst outcome, would it? He'd grab any slice of dominion given him. It would feel bloody wonderful to say no to her this time. Balm for his battered, youthful soul.

"You're plotting, brother of mine, and I know to fear that look. It's the one that occurs before laboratories are destroyed and boats sunk."

Cort shook himself free of the sensation of being swept under by a woman he'd imagined he'd long forgotten. But no. An accidental meeting on a spring afternoon and here he was, dashed and debating his next move.

14

CHAPTER 2

WHERE OPPORTUNITY KNOCKS

*A*lex had done something she'd never done before.

She'd instituted a covert investigation into a man's background for reasons she wasn't fully willing to admit. Curiosity, possibly, and a burning need hidden layers deep. Dangerous any way she played it.

The morning after her chance encounter with Cortland DeWitt, she'd written to her friend, Claudine Grant, seeking information about him. Claudine's husband had served at Waterloo, and it was common knowledge that the late Duke of Herschel's second son had as well. She suspected her friend might know something of him. She and Claudine were part of the Widows' League, a discreet group who discussed controversial topics related to their changed circumstances. They shared advice about navigating a future holding more freedom than most of them had experienced in their lives. When one lost one's husband, situations shifted. Taking a discrete lover, for instance, was not looked upon as severely.

Admittedly, Alexandra was curious about pleasure, about lovemaking. The bliss she'd heard members of the League who'd had satisfactory unions review in closed quarters. Amberly had been neither caring nor skilled. In fact, he'd not been interested, leaving Alexandra to wonder about her husband's proclivities. They hadn't spent much time together after the wedding ceremony, less than six weeks in five years, actually.

Sadly, she hadn't known the man she'd married well.

Hence, her letter from Claudine, two folded sheet of foolscap currently burning a hole in her pocket. What could her friend say that might encourage Alexandra to proposition him? That he'd been an honorable leader, an able fighter, a capable man among men? Maybe she knew everything she needed to after watching Cort ride into the sunset three days ago, his broad body in perfect accord with his mount's. She admired a strong seat on a horse more than most.

Her cheeks flushed when she considered this, but she wanted someone's hands on her. Rough, greedy possession. *Passion.* Her life couldn't be confined to sensual narratives in forbidden books, would it? Her touch in the darkness all she'd be given?

Alexandra halted in the corridor after checking the house before bed, the creak of a loose floorboard sounding beneath her feet. A rake would do nicely, she decided. She'd rarely experienced a spark of attraction as intense as the one she'd felt that day. Her thighs getting as warm as they would if she were standing next to a hearth must mean something. She trailed her slipper through a slice of moonlight settled across the runner.

According to speculation, Cortland DeWitt knew his way around a woman's body. He'd gotten superb marks from those who'd chosen to discuss him in parlors scattered across London. Alexandra had never taken part, of course, but she'd listened, her heart thumping while her body ached.

Why not him? If he was set to be her neighbor again, even for a short period, this presented a fortuitous opportunity. He came from a good family. He was tall. Handsome, more than. His laugh had been delightful. If he was dimwitted, what did it matter? So were most of the men in the *ton*.

It was what he did with his *hands* that counted.

She didn't need his brain. She had a fine one of her own, thank you very much.

As night fell, she headed to her chamber, prepared to read Claudine's letter in bed with a glass of sherry and formulate a plan, as she'd no idea how to seduce a man. She halted on the stair when the knock sounded. A storm had blown through earlier, thunder and rain rattling the windowpanes in their casings. She descended the staircase in alarm. What if something had happened to the horses in the stable? Hamilton, her favorite bay gelding, was sensitive to loud noises.

Alexandra didn't wait for her butler, Cosgrove, to arrive from his suite of rooms in the back of the house. He was sixty if he was a day and moved slower than a three-legged cat. She had the front door open, a humid gust ripping past, before she considered the wisdom of her actions. After all, she was a woman living alone with a small staff of elderly servants, the pistol tucked in her bedside table's top drawer her only means of protection.

Her breath banked in her lungs upon seeing her strapping grooms on the portico's landing, their arms full of Cortland DeWitt.

"What happened?" she breathed and flung the door wide.

The oil sconce's flame flickered wildly as they shuffled into the entryway, the eldest of the grooms, Oscar, kicking the door shut behind them. They had Cort by the shoulders and legs, his head dangling precariously. Alexandra rushed over, sliding her hand into the sodden hair at his nape, supporting his neck as she would a babe's. He had a gash over his left eye that was trailing blood down his jaw, the droplets staining her plank flooring. The wound cut directly through his eyebrow, a mark that would only boost his rakish air. His cravat had been lost, his coat torn at the lapel, his shirt stained crimson and black.

"There's a spare chamber down the hallway," she instructed. "Past the staircase to the left."

"Took a tumble in the squall. We found him alongside the ditch on the main path, just past the bend between Hampton Court and the village. Almost made it to his place, hundred yards from the turnoff. Must have been one of those strikes of thunder that spooked his mount. Duke of Herschel, ain't he? I've seen him around a time or two riding down the lane to his estate."

17

She shook her head, no doubt in her mind. "It's the other one. Cortland."

Oscar squinted, his flaxen brow kicking high. "How can you tell? Word is, they look just alike. Used to trick folks around here with their adventures, they did. Pretending to be one, then the other. Old Mrs. Viceroy said the joke wasn't appreciated by no one."

Alexandra bumped the door open with her elbow and backed into the bedchamber. She didn't know how she knew which brother it was, she simply *knew*. This was the man she'd seen lounging in the courtyard, the one who'd made her skin burn as surely as if he'd dragged his fingertip down her spine.

When they laid him on the bed, his lids quivered and for a brief moment, opened. His eyes were a vivid green, open emerald fields, dazed with pain and confusion. She had not mistaken the color in her memory. She was close enough to note the cusp of gold circling his pupils, making them shine. They really were most stunning.

"Shh..." Alexandra brushed his hair from his brow, lingering, the heat of his skin warming her palm. The thick strands were curling around her fingers from the damp. "You fell from your mount on the post road. I have you."

"Have me," he whispered, so low that only she heard him. Then he blinked twice, his gorgeous eyes closing, lost to the world.

The younger groom, Liam, dropped a leather haversack to the floor. "Found this beside him. It's wet but not ruined. Papers and such inside. Drawings of a mechanical nature. And all his necessary personal items. He wasn't robbed while lying there."

Alexandra glanced up. "His horse?"

"Loyal beast," Liam murmured. "A warmblood, if I'm not mistaken. Cross between an Arab and a draft. Stayed by his side. That's how we saw him as we rode past, truth be told. Holding a good gallop and could have missed them altogether. We settled the animal in the stable. I'll go now and rub him down."

Oscar dusted his hands on his trousers and paced toward the door. "I'll head for the village sawbones, Doc Grover. If I can locate him, as he's down the pub by this time most nights. But knocks to the head

18

can be worrying, so best is best." The young man swallowed, his cheeks coloring. "That is, if you don't need…"

Alexandra adjusted the pillow beneath Cort's head. "I'll wake Cosgrove and have the scullery maid gather hot water and linens. I'm not certain what medicinal supplies we have, but we have something. I haven't had time to review what's here and what I need to purchase on my next trip to London." She waved them off, checking her smile. Benefit number two to being a widow was, nobody tried to protect her from seeing things she'd already seen.

Naked males being one.

She stole a fleeting glance at the man sprawled on her guest bed. Although she'd never seen a physique like this, not once in her life. Her deceased husband had mostly resembled an overripe peach.

When her grooms left the room, Alexandra let her sigh break free. She hadn't wanted to display her concern but head wounds could indeed be problematic. With a trembling hand, she traced her fingertip along the jagged edge of his injury. It wasn't a long cut but it would need stitches, a few, at least. A bruise the size of an apple was forming on his cheek, and he'd winced when they banged his left leg while settling him in the bed.

What if the village physician was already in his cups? What would she do then?

The facts, Alex, stick to the facts.

Cortland DeWitt could not stay in filthy, wet clothing, with an oozing head wound. And if the doctor wasn't steady, she wouldn't allow him to lift so much as a needle. Her crooked stitch was better than a foxed one.

Solving this dilemma was left to her, decisions regarding her childhood tormentor hers.

She swallowed past her apprehension and went in search of supplies and her staff.

It was three hours later before Alexandra had a chance to sit down.

She dragged a threadbare armchair by his bedside and tumbled into it, wilting like a daisy left too long in the sun. Glancing around, she searched for the time. The mantel clock hadn't worked since she was a child and it was stuck at half past three. Which might not be far off, as it was the dead of night. The doctor had come and gone after placing five stitches on Cort's brow and administering warnings about the uncertainty of head injuries. Cosgrove had located clothing suitable for a man a size smaller than their patient, but clean clothing, nonetheless. He'd insisted on disrobing that 'DeWitt scamp'—as he'd referred to Cort—without assistance, grunting and massaging his lower back as he left the room.

She kneaded her own aching back and groaned softly. The room reeked of antiseptic and lilies, the only soap she'd been able to locate. Except for Cosgrove, who only resided in the house when someone was in residence, a man hadn't lived at Hampton Court for going on ten years.

No one since her father.

Alexandra frowned, struggling to place the scent he'd worn. Bergamot, perhaps. Something exacting to match his inflexible demeanor.

After a battle between heart and mind, her gaze found the man tucked in bed, a crisp white sheet settled at his shoulders, the linen allowing a peek at the swatch of hair on his muscular chest. His jaw was heavily whiskered, giving his face a devilish air. If he stayed too long, she'd have to find a way to shave him. His hair had dried, ginger highlights mixed among the curling, mahogany strands. There were groves next to his mouth, earned on the battlefield, she presumed. His lips were parted, muted sighs slipping free to christen the air. His shoulders were straining the seams of the rumpled shirt Cosgrove had wrestled on him.

He'd grown up nicely, with a face one did not easily forget and a body easily coveted.

She couldn't quite believe this dazzling creature was little Cort DeWitt, the boy who'd put a frog in her apron pocket one long ago summer night. Who'd locked her in the conservatory the day of the village festival because she'd threatened to go without him. Who'd tossed pebbles at her window before she'd stormed down to the garden to receive his clumsy kiss.

Before the kiss, she'd never given thought to the fact his actions meant he'd been infatuated with her. Not when there'd been at *least* five years between them, maybe more. Heart thudding a silent tune, she reached, then at the last second, drew her hand back and twisted it in her skirt. This was a man, not a boy. A stranger.

Merely someone she used to know.

Though there were ways to get a glimpse into the mystery.

Shifting, she dug in her pocket, retrieving the letter.

Claudine's handwriting was exquisite, her message concise. And heartbreaking. Astonishingly, her husband had served in the King's Dragoon Guards under Lieutenant Colonel DeWitt. They'd lost half the regiment, including her dear Harold, the highest casualty rate of any calvary unit. Following the battle, the remaining men, under their leader's able direction, had made their way back to safety behind allied lines.

The slice of gossip came next. Lord DeWitt was believed to be the Countess of Rashford's latest conquest, a particular vexation as she'd been Alexandra's cruelest critic that first, beastly season.

Alexandra glanced at Cort between her lashes, then to his haversack resting by the wardrobe. It was partially open, begging entrance. She was on her feet without consideration of what snooping through a man's belongings said about a person, on her knees and digging through the satchel seconds later. DeWitt was stitched above the fold in a faded blue thread. Alexandra traced her finger over the letters, wondering who'd cared enough to personalize the bag in this way. A lover, perhaps.

Her chest burned for no fathomable reason.

She rested the stack of papers she withdrew on her knee. The foolscap was damp and curling at the edges, mechanical sketches as her groom had stated. Quite detailed and elaborate. She tilted her head, studying them closely. An engine of some type, mathematical formulas scattered across the page like a teapot's broken shards across a kitchen floor.

Alexandra pinched the bridge of her nose with a sigh.

If these illustrations were his, Cortland DeWitt's brain was as sturdy as his shoulders. *Blast.* Everyone knew mindless men were easier to control.

"Steam engine," he whispered, the threadbare words jerking her from her musing.

Alexandra jumped up, scattering pages across her slippers.

Cort groaned and closed his eyes, his throat pulling with a tight swallow. From pain or her foolishness, she couldn't say.

She crossed to him, lifting the glass of water from the bedside table. "The physician recommended liquids as soon as you could take them. I'm sorry. I was, that is, your rucksack opened during your accident, unseating your papers and…"

He held up a hand to halt her rambling. Elbowed to a swaying half-sit and grabbed the glass, gulping until she feared he'd heave it back up in his urgency. The shirt Cosgrove had jammed on his shoulders was gaping, the sheet having given way, granting an unparalleled view of his chest right down to his rippled-with-muscle belly. A sliver of one lean hip was exposed as well, drying the last trace of spittle in her throat.

She didn't know what he did to maintain such a physique, but he did something.

Bewildered, she gestured to his drawings spilled across the floor. The ridiculous lie rolled like a spent breath past her lips. "I wanted to see who you were in the event you didn't recall—"

"I don't have amnesia, despite the blow to my head," he whispered against the rim of the glass, his emerald eyes dazed but sharper than the blade of a knife when they met hers. "I know exactly who I am." Then he laughed for reasons she couldn't gauge, collapsing to the bed with a ragged sound, the glass falling from his hand to the mattress. "And exactly who *you* are."

"My grooms found you on the post road." Thinking quickly, Alexandra grabbed the glass before it tumbled to the floor. "With your haversack beside you."

"My horse?"

It pleased her that he'd ask this right off, as she would have. "Being stabled here. He's uninjured. As for you, the village physician placed five stitches on your brow."

Reaching to touch, he grimaced, then dropped his arm to his side. Opening those exquisite green-as-mint eyes, he thankfully kept them off her as he made a thorough study of the chamber. He pointed to the crutch propped against the hearth. "What's that?"

Alexandra gestured to his foot, wrapped tightly with a bandage and propped on a goose down pillow. "It appears you turned your ankle when you lost your seat."

He snorted, clearly disgusted with the situation. "So, I'm stuck here with an aching head and a bum foot. And a clock situated at half past three."

Alexandra smoothed her hand down her bodice. She hadn't expected him to wake until morning, and her gown, besides being wrinkled beyond measure, was one she normally kept for gardening. Her hair, too, had to be a fright. "The doctor recommended bedrest for at least two days. The ankle..." She shrugged and patted the chignon drooping at her nape. Her locks were too heavy to be contained for long. "You may not be able to put weight on it for a bit."

His lips tilted, the internal conversation he was having with himself showing on his face. "And the clock?"

She glanced to the mantel. "Oh, that hasn't worked since—"

"You were a girl," he interrupted, his gaze meeting hers. "I recall her, as a matter of fact." He flicked his hand, his long fingers dancing on the sheet. "Before the viscountess business."

Alexandra allowed herself to examine him as he was examining her. A widow's freedom again providing benefit. She'd never had the opportunity to look upon a man, aside from her husband, with so little clothing on. He didn't blink or twitch so much as a pinkie, merely met her, gaze for gaze. A slight flush lit his cheeks and his hand curled into a fist atop the counterpane but other than that, he permitted her exploration.

The air in the room thickened, awareness bringing a dull ache to her chest. Pressing heat between her thighs, *ah, there*, as if he'd touched her.

How fascinating. How extraordinary. How frightening.

"Alex," he finally said, his voice rusty.

"Cort," she returned faintly, no game left to play.

Blinking hard, he groaned, his lids lowering. "As much as I'd like to continue this little dance, my vision is spotting."

"It's not a dance."

His lips parted on a gentle sigh. "Just wait."

CHAPTER 3

WHERE LIFE TAKES A TURN

*L*ife was amusing as all hell, Cort thought, as he surveyed the parts of the broken clock spread across the scullery's butcher block. A setting, a *woman*, he'd avoided for years, and here he was, right smack in the middle because he'd tumbled off his bloody horse.

He glanced to the intriguing creature kneeling in the flower garden outside the kitchen window. She held a pair of scissors and was selectively snipping what he believed were daffodils, tidying them into a crooked posy she clutched in her fist. The setting sun burrowed through her hair, drawing out auburn highlights in the dusky strands. She'd given up on the sadly constructed knot from the night before, one that hadn't been up to the task of controlling her heavy tresses.

Resting back, she scrubbed her hand across her cheek, likely leaving a dirty smudge. Her next stop was probably the stable to assist Seamus with shoeing horses. A flicker of amusement lit Cort as he imagined what the *ton* would think of the widowed viscountess's hobby—because it could be no more than a hobby.

This is the way he remembered the girl—not that he *wanted* to remember.

Unfussy, clever, exquisite Alexandra Mountbatten.

And, even if she still trifled with horses, she was no longer that chit, no longer holding that name. As for him, Cort didn't quite know who he was anymore. Retired soldier, potential inventor, devoted brother, onetime Lothario. A man in the midst of change. A bloke traveling from one side of his world to the other, sight-unseen.

Some days, a ghost among the living.

The sands were shifting, noticeable even as he disregarded them.

Lifting the clock's mainspring before his eyes, he squinted. Using the bloody crutch he actually needed to keep weight off his throbbing ankle, he looped it through his haversack's canvas strap and dragged the sack across the floor. His spectacles were in a side pocket, hopefully unharmed in the accident.

Fitting them to his face, through corrective lens he noted that the bent coil was the issue. Older clocks incorporated exposed springs versus current timepieces that housed them in metal barrels to prevent twisting. He'd contact his friend, Christian Bainbridge, the foremost watchmaker in England, to get the piece he needed to make the repair. It wouldn't hurt to have Bainbridge visit this estate to service every device in the manor, but that was Lady Amberly's problem, wasn't it?

Cort's problem was convincing his savior to let him return home, in the back of a pony cart if need be, as soon as possible. This situation was more than he could master in a weakened state.

His senses were in overdrive trying to right themselves.

Her enticing scent roamed the air, sinking it's cunning teeth in him. Stronger than the scent of the roasted meat he expected to be served at dinner. The sound of her silky voice as she instructed her staff striking his gut like a shot of whisky. Authoritative yet gentle commands he'd surrender his modest inheritance to hear her use on him. In bed. He'd woken just after dawn to find her slumbering in a tattered armchair she'd drawn close, her wondrous lips parted, her cheek propped shakily, adorably, on her fist.

She'd looked so young, he'd lost his breath for a moment.

Vulnerable, when he didn't think this was the case.

Sweet, when she'd not *once* been nice to him as a lad.

She was only being agreeable now because he'd been dumped, bloody and as cracked as this clock, on her doorstep.

If he'd taken notice of the plump swell of her breasts outlined beneath her atrocious, ill-fitting gown, his shaft rising to pulse in time to his swollen ankle, he hadn't found it in his power to halt the response. In fact, he'd drifted to sleep imagining peeling that faded scrap of satin from her body, unwinding the lopsided knot at her nape, and bringing her to him, his fingers tangled in her hair. Visions of her on her knees, beneath him, rising above.

It was a surprise, considering his medicated condition, that he'd not stained her sheets with a pubescent release.

He gave the spring a spin on the block. Who, he wondered, had undressed him? That ancient crisp of a butler or the chit who'd haunted his dreams since childhood? A chill raced over his skin at the image of her touching him. He dropped his chin to his fist, staring sightlessly into the distance.

He'd prefer being awake if it ever happened again.

At the squeal of the servant's door, he straightened with a grimace. Chanced a glance at his trouser close, indelicacies appropriately hidden. Alexandra didn't wait, however, strolling into the space, her nose jammed in her bouquet. Her gown was vaguely improved over yesterday's selection, faded, but at least, a recognizable shade of blue. The scent of gardenias and daffodils danced in behind her, clouding his wits.

She halted just inside the door, the setting sun at her back, apparently shocked to see him. Her gaze roved his form in an improper manner he recognized, but perhaps she didn't. Had there been a hint of hunger in her eyes? Or was he merely delusional?

With this woman, anything was possible.

She gestured with the posy, sending a golden petal drifting to the floor. "You're repairing my clock. In the kitchen. When you should be in bed."

Ah, he thought, she'd been looking at her timepiece, not at him. *Brilliant.*

He shrugged, trailing his fingertip over a ratchet wheel to add credence to his self-possession. He wasn't bothered by her in the least and wanted her to know it. "I've slept as much as I can. I was going mad in that bedchamber, staring at the rather impressive crack in your ceiling. At some point, Lady Amberly, it will need repair. I thank you most humbly for taking me in last night, but if you could assist, I'd like to arrange transport home. I have the powders from the doctor and will keep off the ankle for another day or two." Although he wasn't at all sure about keeping this promise.

She crossed to him, and before he could move away, took his chin in hand. Tilting his head into the sconce's muted light, she frowned, studying his injury. Her skin was soft against his, the scent of earth and flowers riding the air around her, moving in to catch him by the throat. His breath left him, a clear, helpless shot past his lips.

It had been ages, *eons*, since anyone had touched him for other than self-seeking reasons. Or that he'd allowed it.

"You have working staff there? Someone to help you navigate the stairs and assist with changing your bandage? Is your headache gone? Head wounds are dicey, nothing to laugh off without rest. You need supervision. We had to wake you every hour the first night, if you recall."

Supervision. Bleeding hell, would he like to be supervised by this chit.

Instead, he removed his chin from her grasp before he yanked her across the table and into his lap. "Mrs. Crumley has been with my family since before I was born. We shall manage." He used his impervious tone, his brother's ducal stock and trade. It had worked well in the military, too. And that time he nearly burned down a medieval wing at Cambridge.

Alexandra shook her head and took a small step back—*too* small—still residing in his space. "Mrs. Crumley retired to Derbyshire to live with her daughter."

Cort nudged his spectacles up the bridge of his nose. *Damn.* "Oh, um, yes, I guess I remember that," he said, although he'd no clue what went on two miles down the lane and hadn't cared after Waterloo. For a multitude of reasons, one sitting across from him, he'd avoided

Hampstead like he would the pox. "In any case, someone must be there."

"I don't believe His Grace retains a full staff when he's not in residence." She bumped the posy against her thigh, forcing his gaze where it didn't need to wander. "For mercy's sake, you can't leave your health to a gardener or a groom."

Out of nowhere, a surge of temper whipped through Cort. "His Grace's name is Knox. Remember those boys who chased you around the village? The two who looked so bloody alike they could be twins? Tugging on your braids and hiding insects in your cloak? Two days ago, one of them tumbled off his mount and ended up, bleeding and battered, at your doorstep. A man you chose to pretend you didn't recognize. It would have been entertaining, had I been knocked so brainless I didn't recognize *you* from first sight."

Bracing her hip on the block, Alex grinned, a blindingly beautiful bit of amusement. He'd hated when she laughed at him when they were young. "So that's why you're cross. Because I was caught snooping in your satchel and pretended not to know who you were to hide my humiliation? This was my disgrace, Cort, not yours. It's been years since I've seen you, and I must say"—she gestured the length of him and back with her wilting bouquet—"there've been changes. For one, I've never seen you, even across Swidden's ballroom that time, with spectacles. I barely recognize you as that skinny lad with dirt smeared across his face. Truly, I can't imagine why you'd be vexed with me when I've simply tried to help you."

Why am I vexed, he wondered?

Because I've been in love with you since I was ten years old.

Thrust off his normally-grounded axis, like an arrogant arse, Cort shoved his chair back and surged to his feet. His head swam, a milky haze coloring his vision. He grasped the edge of the block and released a tight breath. Unless he pitched to the ground at her feet, he was leaving this dwelling right bloody *now*. Even if they had to tie him to his mount to keep him in the saddle.

Alexandra was at his side immediately, her arm slipping around his waist as she eased him into the chair. "You're going to hurt yourself. Perhaps this fit of pique is related to your injury. I'll ask the doctor when he returns tomorrow morning."

Cort rested his spectacles on his brow and scoured his fist across his eyes. He wanted to laugh. Knox would have. *Fit of pique.* Men did not have fits of *pique.* They suffered violent outbursts and engaged in drunken brawls. They did not sulk or pout.

Ignoring his hysteria, his torment went about preparing tea, the rattle of a cup and saucer when she delivered the beverage sounding before him.

"Drink," she said, settling across from him.

He blinked to find her gaze fixed upon him, the bouquet resting by her side. Her eyes were an unforgettable color, a dusky violet he'd never encountered on another living soul. So light he'd often imagined he could see through them and into her soul. A place he'd wanted to access so badly he could taste it. Those immature fancies where one supposed strong sentiments must, simply *must*, be returned. Cort knew better. Because one felt an emotion didn't mean the emotion was actually there. He'd love to tell her that his childhood obsession had evaporated like morning mist the moment he'd left this place. Even if it wasn't true.

Gathering his strength, he rested back, cradling the cup in his hands. English to his core, the tea—chamomile, he determined from a sniff—calmed him as he sipped. Even as the daring chit across from him made his pulse race.

"I sent a missive to your brother so he wouldn't worry." Alexandra reached for a lemon scone she'd brought with the tea and bit into it with relish. He wasn't going to think about the crumbs clinging to her bottom lip. He *wasn't.*

Smiling, she nudged the plate his way.

He grabbed one, the taste of citrus hitting his tongue with a burst. *Hmm...they were bloody good.* "I wish you hadn't. He takes the elder brother routine seriously, and then some. A few minutes older, though he values it as three hundred years." Reaching, he took another scone and polished it off in two bites, chewing as he added, "He'll send his personal physician if he thinks I'm not getting appropriate care.

I'm warning you now, lest they knock on your door in the middle of the night."

She licked a morsel from the edge of her mouth, pitching his stomach to his knees. "What sent you from your mount and into that ditch? You were the most capable rider in Hampstead at one time, able to handle any horse Seamus put before you. I assumed it was the storm."

He sipped, eyeing her over the rim, shocked she'd noticed a damned thing about him back then. "It wasn't the storm." She wanted honesty, did she? Well, Cort didn't like to give and not *get*. His negotiating expertise in the military had been legendary. "What do I receive in return for cooperating with this line of questioning?"

She frowned, a charming dent, almost deep enough to be called a dimple, winking from the plump curve of her cheek. "Are you proposing a trade?"

She was fearless, he'd hand her that, another trick of memory coming to him about the girl. She'd not once backed down that he recollected. "I must be mad-bored, my mind still muddled from the accident, but I suppose I am. I offer this, your honesty for my own. But I want an admission you wouldn't share with anyone else. Top shelf details or it's no deal."

Her pupils flared, curiosity and a spark of something he couldn't define making them shine like agate. "Is that what you'll give? Something no one else knows?"

He dipped his chin in agreement, wondering if the blow to his head had truly rendered him senseless. "I will."

"Why?"

He reached for another of her delightful scones and tore into it. "For the same reason I do most things, because I want to."

"That must be nice," she whispered, so softly she thought he hadn't heard.

"Isn't that the way it is for you? Freedom, now that you're widowed?"

"Freedom for a woman in this world?" She laughed and plucked at her posy as petals drifted to the floor. "You must be joking. We're bound by society's dictates until the day we die."

He raised a brow, chewing slowly. "I assume you want me to go first."

Charmingly discomfited, she shifted on her chair. "It was your idea."

"Indeed, it was." He laughed, a tad rusty but real. His amusement of late had been as thin as lace, punched through with thousands of tiny holes. Nerves were present, he'd admit, swirling in his belly. He'd not told anyone about the episodes, not even Knox. His brother worried enough already.

Picking up a balance wheel, Cort spun it between his fingers, focusing on the tarnished metal rather than the keen glimmer in her eyes. "Someone was hunting in the parklands I was passing through. That lonesome stretch before you reach the village. Rain had begun to fall but it was light, not hard enough to muck up the roads yet. I'd picked up speed to get to the estate before the downpour when there was the discharge of a rifle somewhere off to my left."

He paused, his heartbeat kicking, the piquant scent of blood washing through him. *Memories, Cort, they're only memories.* Swallowing, he prayed his voice sounded composed before the lone person with the probable power to bring him to his knees. "Certain sounds have the ability to send me back to the battlefield. Unfortunately, a carriage wheel thumping over a cobble or glass shattering upon ballroom marble deliver me directly to Waterloo. It's been a challenge to return to normal life when my life is no longer normal."

He glanced at her then, drawn and repelled by the sympathy in her gaze, but hardened enough from a turbulent past to withstand both. "So, my little secret, the storm had nothing to do with my being tossed from my mount. It was the gunshot that spooked the rider, not the horse."

Silence became a living thing, roaming the kitchen like a viscous fog. Cort exhaled too noisily for comfort and sank back. *There,* he thought, he'd told someone and survived the telling. The next time, with Knox, would be easier. It was on his list when he could muster the courage.

Alexandra fiddled with a hydrangea bloom. "They say you're attached to Countess Rashford."

His gaze tracked back to her, when he'd been desperately searching the space for a bottle of something stronger than tea to wash away the vaguely unpleasant taste of honesty. "Who is 'they'?"

She plucked a pale blue petal from its stem and twisted it between her fingers, sending a spicy, floral aroma into the air. "The society pages."

"Scandal rags, you mean."

She shrugged a delicate shoulder, her cheeks flushing.

He reached for another scone, beginning to enjoy this encounter now that his pulse was slowing, allowing his brain to step into play. "What could my dalliances possibly have to do with your part of our bargain?"

"You're a known entity. Safe." The words came out in a rush.

He paused, mid-bite. "Meaning?"

"I know you. Or I used to. Your family." She drew the petal along a jagged scar in the wood, her gaze dancing away. "I'm part of a group—"

"The Wicked Widows."

Her lips tightened, the first sign of vexation she'd shown. "That's a senseless name created by senseless people. We're nothing close to wicked."

He laughed, unable to contain his mirth. "The same senseless folk who write those gossip columns you're relying upon for your information about me."

She huffed, crushing the petal in her fist. "As I was saying, I'm part of a group that has...progressive views regarding a widow's future. Most, unless they're in dire financial straits, don't wish to marry again, unless it was an exceptional experience the first time. Perhaps that is wicked in the *ton's* eyes. We want independence, not the amount a man has, of course, but rather, what we paid our marital membership dues to obtain."

A hum of interest, the same illuminating her eyes, powered through him. Now they were getting somewhere. "Your marriage wasn't exceptional, I take it?"

She shook her head, her throat bobbing with a stiff swallow. "Therefore, I'm curious. That is my honest admission to you. My part of the wager."

"Curious," he murmured, his body burning at the prospect of answering any questions she had. "About what"—he pointed to her, then tapped his chest—"happens between a man and a woman?"

"About the pleasurable part."

Cort paused, astonished to realize how long it had been since someone surprised him. He wasn't used to feeling much of anything anymore. He shifted, hoping his swelling cock wouldn't expose his sudden attention. Not yet. This game, he understood, must be handled with diplomacy. "And a safe man such as myself could be the answer?"

She plucked another petal and gave it a twirl, her boldness beginning to impress him. "Your reputation is tainted but typical. The rumor being that you know what to do when called upon to do it. More than know, you're good at it. When not all men are." Her violet gaze caught his, her smile six shades of devious shyness. "Women gossip in those parlors we're relegated to while the men adjourn to cards and billiards and drink. That, and stitch landscapes."

Cort glanced into his empty teacup, gathering his thoughts as he read the sodden leaves sticking to the bottom—which he could not do while gazing upon the woman spitting dares across from him.

She likely wanted nothing but a kiss. A *simple* show of the delight that could be found between the sexes. He nudged his spectacles when they slipped down his nose, thinking hard.

When was the last time he'd kissed a woman for the basic but heady pleasure of it?

"Never mind, I'll find someone else. It's a ridiculous proposal."

He looked up sharply. *Oh, no, you won't.* Aside from his enjoyment, this could be a way to remove the illusion that had been sitting like a toad on his chest since boyhood. Of the perfect woman. When there was no perfect woman. The genuine article was never as good as a

34

fantasy, and it was time to prove it. "It's a sensible suggestion to test the waters with a friend, of sorts. A childhood acquaintance. Someone harmless," he added, when he'd never once thought of himself as harmless, and neither had anyone else. "I suppose, I'm safe in that way."

She smoothed her hand down her bodice in a charming show of nervousness. "Once you're healthy, that is."

His body pulsed, his breath snagging in his throat. "I'm healthy now, Alex."

For this, a man was always healthy. Scooting his chair back to make room for her, he nodded to the crutch propped against the block. "I would come to you, run to you, but as it is…"

He hadn't meant to admit he'd run to anyone, but there it was. More damned honesty. She seemed to easily pull it from him.

They stared, the air heating faster than it would if they'd tossed dry kindling on the hearth. He could hear his heartbeat in his ears, flowing down his arms and into his fingertips. It felt good. He felt more alive than he had in months, years.

Will she? Won't she? Then she was shoving to her feet and crossing to him while his blood simmered in his veins.

Bloody hell.

It looked like he was finally going to get a taste of his youthful obsession. He could only hope this severed Alexandra Mountbatten from his mind, once and for all.

CHAPTER 4

WHERE A KISS CHANGES EVERYTHING

*A*lexandra was tired of listless kisses.

She'd had a lifetime of unskilled efforts on sorrowfully moonlit verandas. And later, her attempts with an indifferent spouse.

She wanted to bet on a winning horse this time.

If kissing Cortland DeWitt was a gamble, so be it. What better way to find out if the inadequacies in her marriage had been her fault than to attach herself to one of the Trio's lips? Perhaps she wasn't suited to the act, sparking a fire in a man an impossible endeavor. Wasn't it best she recognize this before spending the rest of her life wondering?

She'd never sparked anything in Viscount Amberly, that was certain.

"Quit thinking and get over here, sweetness."

Sweetness. Of course, he said this to everyone. But it warmed her, nonetheless, because she was weak.

Alexandra halted just out of reach. Before she committed fully to this wager, she allowed herself a moment to take him in. When she'd stumbled into the deserted scullery off the kitchen, it was to find her injured visitor seated at her scuffed butcher's block, an introspective expression on his face, parts of her mantel clock scattered before him. Her breath had raced right out of her because she'd never seen him like this. Never realized how attractive he was. Spectacles balanced on the bridge of the most patrician nose in England, rumpled shirtsleeves rolled high on his forearms, his hair mussed about his jaw in disordered waves the color of the cocoa she drank every morning. A stark, white bandage contrasting against his sun-kissed skin.

A mix between a scholar and a scoundrel, the most enticing vision imaginable.

As if he read her thoughts, his sleepy, green gaze met hers. His lips twitched in a near smile, clever and knowing. An earthy scent, leather and the floral fragrance from her soap, drifted to her on a passing breeze sneaking in the open window.

She changed her mind right there.

Cort DeWitt wasn't merely attractive, he was gorgeous.

He tilted his head, his spectacle lenses shimmering in the oil lamp's glow. "Are you reneging on the agreement before we've even begun?"

"No," she whispered and moved closer, pleased when his smile flattened, his fingers clenching into a fist on his knee. Her pulse kicked, her heartbeat scattering. Incredibly, with his gaze lighting a fire inside her, she understood this meant she wanted him.

And possibly, joyfully, he wanted her.

Closing the distance, she stepped between his spread legs. She wasn't allowing her attention to drift lower than his belly as she wasn't sure how to handle what she'd find.

Bracing her knee on the chair, she leaned in, removing his spectacles and placing them on the block. His breathy sigh streaked through her, piercing like a dart in the tight space between her thighs. Giving her courage to go further. His lids fluttered, thankfully relieving her of drowning in the sea-green beauty of his gaze. The muted light revealed the amber tips of his lashes, the pale scar on his jaw, the freckle above his top lip.

She wanted to devour him, when she'd never wished to devour a man before.

So this is what desire feels like, she thought in wonder.

Gripping the arm of the chair, she didn't wait for Cort to touch her. The honest admission had been his idea—the kiss was hers. His lips were firm but silky-smooth when she brushed her mouth across them. His dense stubble a fascinating disparity. The whisper of his breath across her cheek pulling her in, his lips parting to invite her.

He released a soft, knee-melting moan, his arm coming around her waist, palm pressed to her lower back, sending her in a gentle spill against him. Her breasts flattened to his chest, her arms having nowhere to go but around his neck. Gravity and passion took over until she was kneeling before him, erasing any sweet tentativeness.

Her lips opened, her tongue following his in a dance that quickly spiraled into more than she'd imagined in her grandest dreams. No one had dared kiss her like this.

Her hand fisted in the silky hair at the nape of his neck, her other going to clutch his shoulder. Seeking more, he cradled her jaw, slanting her head, guiding her. Groaning when he found what he was looking for—which was the deepest, most consuming experience of her life. She fought the sensation of falling as her toes curled in her slippers, the needy sound lancing the air one she feared was coming from her.

With a choked exhalation, he pulled back, letting a breath of air slide between them. Chest heaving, his gaze captured hers. There was a hint of anger on his face that, strangely, only made her want him more. Conceivably, it was better if he felt more than he cared to.

Better for her anyway.

Seconds clicked by as if her broken clock was counting off time. Cort's eyes had colored a cavernous, lake-bottom green, his jaw tensing as he swallowed. He whispered what sounded like an oath, tunneled his hand into the hair at her crown, then his mouth was hard and hot on hers. His tongue circling, fencing, in battle.

Fighting her. Or himself.

She stumbled and he lifted, bringing her to sit on his lap.

Where everything she'd not wished revealed suddenly *was*. His shaft, firm and long beneath her bottom, evidence of his need. She had to keep her hands occupied, woven in his hair, tangled in his shirt, to keep from touching him there. He clutched her hip, fingers curving in possession and drawing them into a negligible but convincing dance. A sensual grind reminiscent of the push and pull of sexual congress. This, she recognized.

"Alex," he murmured against her lips, her name drawn out in a ragged whisper.

She could only hum, wiggle, sigh. *Yes, yes, yes,* if he was asking.

Yanking her skirt to her waist, he shifted her until his leg was wedged between hers. Her body shimmered, fevered, her skin heating, sweat breaking out in a fine line along her lower back. A cascade of pleasure rippled through her, racing forth like sunlight as he began to move her atop his muscled thigh. Incredibly, the beginnings of an orgasm roared within reach. By her own hand, and her own hand *only*, she recognized this feeling.

In the span of one second, the kiss spun into another realm.

She swayed, her lips leaving his to trail down his jaw, biting and sucking as he urged her into a fury, riding his leg, the most erotic act outside *the* act she'd ever performed. She'd lost what was left of her inhibitions and her mind. His hand slid low, curving around her bottom, moving her even more suitably from this vantage point. His groan flowed down her throat and into the pit of her stomach. *Oh, to be touched like this.* With such hunger and need.

It was heaven for a woman who'd gone so long without. Gone forever without.

Her nipples tightened, her corset a severe restriction when she wanted to be free of every restraint. For once in her bloody life, *free*.

"My bedchamber," Alexandra whispered into the moist patch of skin beneath his ear. His whiskers were dense and grainy against her tongue, her seeking lips.

He halted, his hand having made it halfway from her hip to her breast, where she'd imagined it curving around the plump globe and squeezing until she melted into a puddle on her planked scullery floor. They were sensitive and had never been given enough attention.

Blinking as if he was coming out of a coma, his gaze struck hers, his expression adorably confounded. "Your bedchamber," he mouthed in endearing repetition.

She licked her lips, delighted when his pupils flared, sparks of gold flaring in mossy green. "Where we can do more, Cort." As in, *more*. Naked, blissful, screaming more. Destroyed bed and ripped sheets more.

Fantasy bits she now imagined might be possible after all.

He shook his head and moved her an inch away, not an inch closer. A grating slide down his hard thigh that didn't ease the storm brewing inside her. "I thought..." He exhaled, struggling. "When you, this, that you meant..." He frowned, recovering, a hard edge entering his eyes. His bandage had come loose on one side and was dangling over his eyebrow. "No, oh, *no*," he whispered and hoisted her off his lap.

She stumbled into the block, reaching to gain her balance, her skirt dropping with a wispy lament around her ankles. An uneasy ripple coursed through her, though she managed to keep her tone steady. Successfully hiding the feral beat of her heart, her racing pulse. "Is this not what you wanted?"

Cort scrambled to retrieve his crutch, jammed it under his armpit and rose shakily to his feet. As this was the first time she'd stood this close to him since he'd left for boarding school—he'd either been sitting, unconscious or across a ballroom the other times—she was shocked to realize how tall he was. How broad of shoulder and chest. A stubbled jaw and an expression fit for a vexed god, he looked more like a brigand than a man of society.

Honestly, like the lemon scones, he looked good enough to eat in two tasty bites.

"I'm confused," she said because, truly, she was. Three-quarters of the way to pleasure, and he'd stopped? She'd invited him to her bedchamber, albeit not very tactfully, and he was saying *no*? His shaft was tenting his trousers, so arousal wasn't the issue. She was leagues out of practice enticing a man. "Why are you leaving?"

Cort tapped his temple, grimacing as he inadvertently grazed his wound. "This kiss was supposed to get you out of here, not embed you deeper." He yanked the bandage free and tossed it to the floor before beginning a wobbly circle of the scullery. Definitely an agile man, the crutch nonetheless presented a laborious journey. He made it to the window, where he stood staring out, his shoulders rising and falling.

She heard him mumbling beneath his breath but couldn't make out the words.

Alexandra had the sudden understanding that she was dealing with more than a kiss. Men could, she knew, be sensitive creatures. "I'm missing something."

He glanced over his shoulder, flashing a hostile smile. "You always have, Lady Amberly."

She thought back to their childhood. Cort had visited Hampton Court more than Knox, always underfoot, always teasing. Napping in the stable loft, stealing oranges from the conservatory, volumes from her father's library. Too young for her, of course, a lad in leading strings when she'd been well out of the nursery. Nevertheless, he'd been persistent, trailing behind, seeking attention. And there'd been that kiss, brief and awkward, before he left. Why, he'd been no more than fourteen or so then.

Like the flare of a matchstick, the answer came to her.

She coughed, a delighted peal of laughter rolling past her lips, amusement she should have stifled. "The boy was enamored with me, and the man is discomfited. Goodness, Cort, why be embarrassed? I was little more than a silly, young fool myself."

At her words, he was across the chamber before she could stop him, placing more weight on his injured leg than he should, pushing through the doorway and stalking unevenly down the corridor, the crutch tapping the floor in angry pops.

"I'm not laughing at you, it's more startled surprise!" She took her skirt in hand and raced to catch him. "The kiss was lovely." Lovely? Dear heaven, it had been *magical*. Her feet were inches off the ground still, her skin aflame, her knees beyond weak. Perhaps, if she handled him gently, he'd accept her offer to see her bedchamber. Glide beneath her sheets, between her thighs, and do wicked things to her. "Cort, wait, stop!"

But he didn't hesitate, his long-legged stride taking him swaying down the hallway.

For the first time in history, her butler, Cosgrove, materialized from the shadows when she'd rather he remain hidden. He likely suspected the antics that had been going on in the scullery. "My lord, how may I be of assistance?"

"I need to return to Herschel House immediately. I have business affairs to attend to. Repairs to the roof. And something else I can't recall at the moment. Rotting planks in one of the parlors. Or maybe it was the library." Scowling, he snapped his lips shut.

Cosgrove flicked his gloved fingers in pithy reply. "Of course. We'll have the groom ride alongside on your horse so he is returned with you. One moment, please, sir." Then he was gone, the front door closing behind him, presumably to gather her groom and carriage. She hated to tell the seething man beside her that her butler didn't move quickly.

Alexandra pleated the frilled edge of her sleeve between her fingers. "Your clothing. Your rucksack. Your drawings."

He grunted, fiddling with the crutch, his gaze shifting to the ceiling, the floor, anywhere but her. "Send them to me. I'm the next manor down the lane, in case you've forgotten. I won't have time to work on the designs until tomorrow."

"Steam engines."

His gaze sharpened, a charming furrow settling between his brows. His eyes were glowing as brightly as freshly cut grass, but he wasn't up to sharing their beauty with her.

She shrugged, her cheeks going hot. When had a man last unsettled her? Vauxhall Gardens, 1812? "You mentioned them when you were brought in. I was digging through your personal effects." An incident she might have been better off letting him forget. Alexandra realized she was interested if she was using talk of steam engines to keep him from leaving. It wasn't her best delay tactic, but it was better than nothing.

"Did I say anything else?"

"Something about our conversation being a dance. When I stated it wasn't one, you said, 'just wait.'"

Anchoring himself on the crutch, he scrubbed his hand over his chin. Laughing, he muttered, "I bet I did. Out of my head foolishness."

"You had feelings for me." For some reason, she needed to know.

Wanted to know. "And, somehow, due to ignorance on my part, I've hurt yours."

Finally, his gaze clashed with hers, his jaw flexing. His fingers closed about the scuffed grip of his crutch until she feared the wood would shatter into twigs. "Waterloo wasn't as painful as this inquiry, my lady. And war isn't pleasant."

"Alex," she murmured, staring at his lips in the hopes he'd press them to hers again. The top one rolled over the bottom in some sort of masculine non-reply. A simple gesture that ignited her blood again. "You called me Alex before. No one outside Hampstead calls me such, but here, it's who I am. How I think of myself."

The clatter of a carriage rolling up the drive echoed through the open door. "My clock," Alexandra gestured to the scullery. "You're going to leave me with it in pieces spread over my butcher's block?" *Leave me with this quivering sensation in my belly? Between my thighs? All because you had a boyish crush I didn't know about?*

He glanced to the door, sensing freedom, then back at her. "I'll send the part it requires. A casing for the spring. Anyone with a mind for mechanics can repair it for you."

"Fine," she ground out, getting angry herself. "I'll send your possessions at dawn. Race into the twilight, will you."

He exhaled through his teeth. Then he was before her, her chin tipped high by the finger he slipped beneath it. Leaning over her, he seized her lips without explanation, without hesitation. With fury in his touch, confusion, *desire*. In seconds, they were tangled up, tongues and lips, teeth and hands. Her fingers clutching his shoulders, holding him steady, holding herself steady.

She was amazed how quickly she was learning what he liked, what she needed.

Finally, someone understood her in this way when she was only coming to understand herself.

And he was leaving.

Backing away, tipping an imaginary hat, and striding unevenly through her door.

CHAPTER 5

WHERE REGRET ENTERS THE
CONVERSATION

*H*e was a fool.

A temperamental arse. An idiot.

He'd rejected a woman he desperately desired because of hurt *feelings*? Had he really done that? Cort DeWitt, profligate Lothario, experienced champion of the one-night adventure? What in the everloving hell was wrong with him? Alex had invited him to her bedchamber after he'd kissed her like his life depended upon it, and he'd stormed out without another word?

Her eyes had been filled with longing, and he'd left her there, alone with it? A chit he imagined had been alone for a very long time.

With a curse, Cort tossed his correspondence to the desk in what had once been his father's study and was now Knox's. And his, he supposed. The three minutes between the brothers weren't a familial division as they shared everything but the title. The room still smelled faintly of the select brand of cheroots his father had imported from Spain. Citrusy, with a touch of lemon riding the dull aroma of tobacco.

His heart thumped hard to recall that it had been almost a year since his father's passing, four months after his return from Waterloo. Cort would never have forgiven himself if he'd returned with both his parents gone. His mother had been taken from them when he was just shy of twenty—he, Knox and Damien, thankfully, at her bedside—and those last seconds of her life were his most painful to date. His father had mercifully died in his sleep.

In a vile mood, Cort rifled through his missives, bypassing everything from formal invitations he'd no intention of accepting to Countess Rashford's benevolent offer to visit Hampstead to assist him in his 'time of need.' Through the domestic's communication wire, the speediest channel in England, his ridiculous accident was now known to everyone in society. Another escapade to add to his list.

Despite his wish for the previous night to be scrubbed away, a flash of memory fired his senses. Alex's plump breasts pressed to his chest, her throaty little moans piercing his resistance. Desire curled low and hot in his belly. The vision of lifting that soft flesh to his waiting mouth, his lips wrapping around her peaked nipple and sucking until she cried out, washed over him like a wave.

His engine designs lay forgotten at his side, his ankle throbbing in time to the pulse in his cock. He was going to chafe his skin if he took himself in hand again, which would make thrice. More than he'd played with himself in one day since he was a greedy lad.

He glanced to the countess's letter with a leaden heart.

He didn't want her.

He wanted the woman whose kiss made him misplace his words. The girl who'd had him yearning when he'd no idea what yearning meant. Only that the sight of her had been sunshine lighting his soul.

He knew what Alex desired. One night and one night only.

When one night was his standard bargain. Her group of widows were known to reject closer associations. Freedom came with a price. Why this unspoken arrangement discomfited him, he was terrified to contemplate.

Cort had never brought emotion into his liaisons. Not once.

Body at the ready, heart locked behind closed doors.

However, could he deny Alexandra Mountbatten, deny himself, out of fear? He could give her what she coveted and pray—*pray*—the experience absolved him. Like a razor across stubble, removing his need for her. Because he genuinely believed fantasies never lived up to the real thing. After all, she'd been his dream since 1800 or so.

But their kiss had been blinding. A kiss for the ages. All he'd imagined and more.

What did *that* say about his theory?

He shoved from the chair before he could talk himself out of it. Grabbing that bloody crutch and heading into the night before he admitted that adoration wasn't an easy emotion to disregard.

Alexandra stared into the darkness, the scent of the delphiniums and orchids beneath her bedchamber window drifting inside on a careless breeze. She'd helped Seamus all afternoon with a temperamental gelding, and she should have been so tired she'd fall directly into bed. Instead, here she stood, gazing sightlessly into the distance, in the direction of the Duke of Herschel's estate. Over the parkland-steeped vista, she could make out the peak of a chimney if she squinted.

A gust of air streaked past, shaking the lanterns glimmering in the garden below. The chill tunneled through her nightgown's thin silk, making her shiver.

And that's when she saw him.

The crutch was unmistakable, as was his lumbering stride snaking through the shadows. A dark cape billowed behind him, giving him a sinister look when she didn't, in actuality, think there was a sinister thing about him, aside from a slightly brooding nature. His smile came easily, the grooves aside his mouth testament to them arriving often. He was kind to his staff (fact) and to his paramours (rumor). He was also a capable soldier and a loyal brother.

When she wished to know the man.

Heart hammering, Alexandra turned to rest her bottom on the window ledge, waiting for him to come to her. He'd find a way inside the dwelling—she didn't doubt his lockpicking skills, if it came to that —and it wasn't long before she heard his uneven footfalls in the passage outside her chamber. Her door was ajar, and her pulse gave a leap when it swung wide.

He limped into the room, his smile a thousand shades of diffident boldness. His gaze roved the length of her, *twice*, before his eyes met hers. They were hot, a bright, burning green.

"You can't just break into someone's home, Cortland DeWitt. Enter my bedchamber when you haven't been invited."

With a twist of his lean body, he snicked the door closed using that infernal crutch of his. Looking like he'd been born to the sport of seduction, which feasibly, he had. "I was invited."

She snorted, unable to suppress it. Her mother had hated that sound. *Uncouth girl,* she'd been called more than once. Maybe tonight, she would prove her mother right. "That was yesterday's offer. Withdrawn, I might add."

As he crossed to her, she recorded the rise in temperature, awareness charging the air. When he stood before her, his lips tilting in a half-smile, her ire kicked up a notch. He'd let his cape drift to the floor on the way over—as if he meant to stay. Had been asked to stay.

Damn the man, anyway. Arrogant toad.

Amused, he trailed his knuckle down her cheek, a trail of fire following his passage. "Don't be cross with me, sweetness. I'm here to ask for another chance."

She stared into his eyes, hating that she could see everything. Remorse, hunger, the gilded flecks at the outer edge of his pupil highlighting what she imagined was a hint of apprehension. The delightful boy melding with the vexing man. She gripped the ledge to keep from launching herself into his arms. The moment felt significant for reasons she feared.

She wasn't falling for one of the Troublesome Trio. She *wasn't.*

Leaning, he grazed his lips over her jaw. "Are you going to make me beg?"

Her breath caught. "Would you?"

Nipping the skin beneath her ear, he brought her to her feet, sighing against her skin when her husky moan slipped free. "For one night with you, I'd beg. Happily. I was out of my bloody mind to deny you before. Forgive me."

One night. An encounter with an established expiration date.

Her heart sank even as longing rushed through her. He didn't want more. Would not expect her to change her life for him. A rule of the Widow's League, in fact. This was a game he'd played a hundred times, a thousand, with glowing reviews. He knew how to manage an affair, and she wanted to have one.

Take him, Alex. Let him show you how it's done.

"I accept your apology," she whispered, her head dropping back as he began to make love to her in a way no man ever had. Whispered suggestions, commands, pleas, his ardor warming her soul. His broad body surrounding hers, a promise of more.

A promise of everything.

Bracing his fist on the ledge, his crutch clattered to the floor. Guiding her mouth to his, he took her lips, sinking into a bruising kiss that jumped in exactly where the other had left off. Engulfed in sensation, yearning, lust. His arm wound around her waist, tugging her against him. Firm muscle twitched beneath her seeking hands. Shoulder, waist, hip. Fingers tangling in his hair, guiding the kiss. Finally, taking a measure of control.

"That's it," he whispered and backed her into the wall, caging her in. He cupped her breast, his thumb circling her nipple as reason left her in a rush. "Take what you want."

Submission and power twisted through her, contradictory needs perfectly wedded.

Rampant passion—without limit, without fear—colored the moment, a wash of crimson staining her sight. Alexandra had never felt truer to her body, truer to herself. She'd not known how to ask for what she desired or had a man willing to *let* her ask.

Cort DeWitt allowed all, his kindness claiming not only her ardor but part of her heart.

With a gentle spin, he backed her toward the bed, his step stumbling but determined. His breath scattered against her cheek, his grip demanding, his shaft stiff at her hip.

"Cort," she gasped when they reached their destination. "Wait."

He lifted his head, his eyes shining like tarnished copper in the muted lamplight. The loveliest shade they'd ever turned in her presence. His cheeks were flushed, his lips swollen from her consideration, proof of his need should she require it. "I don't want to wait. I've been waiting for ten years," he growled and turned to sit on the mattress, taking his weight off his leg with a sigh. Thumbing the short row of buttons on her nightgown free, he let the material gape, his gaze so mad with yearning, she shivered from the heat of it. "I'll lay my proposal before you, should you have any objections."

Nudging silk aside, exposing her breast, he caressed her hardened nipple. "I plan to suck on these until you can't stand, not another second." Making good on his vow, his mouth covered one peak, his cheeks hollowing. The sight of him drawing her between his lips, his tongue coming out to lick, did something horrid and wonderful to her.

"I never liked this before," she admitted in a ragged whisper, tangling her fingers in his hair and directing him to the other starved-for-attention bud.

But *this*, oh…

How had she not known how brilliant this could feel?

He trailed his nose round the plump curve, his teeth nipping and sending another ripple of pleasure dancing along her skin. "The wrong man, perhaps."

Perhaps, she thought and tumbled into the thrill of being seduced.

Gripping her hip, he drew her closer. "Then I'm either going to raise this slip of silk high or tear it completely from your body." Going with the former, he drew her nightgown in fistfuls until she stood nude to the waist before him. He looked down, a tattered exhalation streaking free. "Christ, you're beautiful. I should have known. The hair between your legs is a shade lighter than the glory on your head. My weakness, right there. Enslaved and desperate at the sight."

"I'm surprised you'll readily admit this to me."

"I can't very well hide it, sweetness." Exhaling through his teeth, his gaze caught hers. With a crooked smile, he gave the nightgown a tender tug. "This has to go. *Please*. I'll leave the destruction of clothing for the next session." He laughed, charming her. "And if you're wondering, this is the DeWitt version of begging."

Next session. Did that mean they'd touch each other more than one time during the night? She and Amberly had spent ten minutes at a maximum making love and not more than thrice a year, almost by calendar date, for their entire marriage.

Alexandra experienced a moment's panic. This was it, decision made if she disrobed. With a drawn breath, she stepped back, nudged the nightgown from her shoulders and wiggled until it lay in a puddle at her feet.

Cort held back, tension radiating through his biceps and shoulders. His knuckles paled where his fingers lay knotted in the counterpane. "You are a wonder. One I've been waiting my entire life to see."

She blushed, amazed he'd held such adulation for her, and she'd not realized it.

Leaning back, he grazed his hand over his cock, which was straining powerfully against his trouser close. Flipping one button, then the next, he grinned. A wicked, calculating tilt of his lips. "I've not been so hard for so long—practically every second for two days—since I was a callow lad. I thought I took care of myself enough times to ease the ache. Apparently, three isn't the magic number."

"*Three*," she murmured, fascinated. She'd never seen a man caress himself in this manner. It was the most erotic act she'd ever witnessed.

His trousers gaping, he worked his shaft from his drawers. When his rigid length sprang free, Alexandra blinked, her tongue hitting the back of her teeth. *Oh...*

He gave his cock a languid stroke before looping his arm about her waist and drawing her into the vee of his spread legs. He shifted his hand between her thighs, parting her folds in delicate but unmistakable possession. "The choice is yours," he said and slid his finger inside her, pumping until she gasped, her core going damp and hot, the world fading into the shadows. "Either you climb atop me and we go that way, you riding, quickly, a first shot to relieve us both. Or you lay back and I go slowly, until *you're* begging for mercy. Or, hell, until I'm begging, as I said I would."

"I want both," she stated in a rush.

His brow lifted, the cut slicing through it branding him as something other than a duke's son. "That matches my thoughts perfectly."

His patient regard giving her courage, she didn't hesitate, cradling his jaw as she fastened her lips to his. Climbing atop him was quite easy without clothing, her knees wedging beside his hips. Like mounting a horse, only better. She couldn't believe she wasn't intimidated by her nudity, but she wasn't. This man made her feel fearless and free.

The anticipation of feeling him was nothing compared to the reality of his shaft sliding inside her in a slow, molten burn. Inch by inch by inch. He brought the kiss into the production, his hips moving in tandem, rising to meet her downward thrusts, until he was embedded fully. His hand swept her body, cupped her breast, testing the weight of the globe in his palm. "I'll go gently. Until you're prepared."

"I don't need gentle. I need *you*." She wasn't a virgin. She yearned for what was coming.

The declaration lit a fire beneath him.

She knew what to do, mostly, from imagination more than experience, lifting while he guided. Elemental, really. Her hand went to the flexing muscles of his upper back, clutching as he stroked with tormented moans of pleasure. His touch became urgent, branding her, his need spoken without restraint. With artistry, he drew her leg high over his hip, thrusting deeply as they moved together.

She couldn't soften the animalistic sounds leaving her lips, streaking past his ear and into the night. The dance was clumsy and wild and wonderful. A cadence found, then lost, then found again. Plunging, cresting, swelling. Bodies bumping. Her nails digging into his skin, his teeth at the nape of her neck. Kisses broken, words frayed and tattered. The air alive with the resonance of their bliss.

The tingling sensation started in her toes and rushed north, taking her breath with it. Close, she was close.

He halted, his grip firm on her waist, his brow going to hers and pressing. Moist skin to moist skin, hot breath to hot breath. "Don't move. Don't. Move." Though his cock shifted inside her even as he said this. "If you do, I won't last."

She squirmed, searching, the nub of her sex throbbing, ready to send her off a pleasure cliff. "I thought this was...our first shot. A quick exploration." Then she glided her mouth beside his ear and sighed inside it, "I'm there, darling. Bring me home."

He growled and tightened his hold on her. "I can help you...help me."

She laughed weakly, teasing him, an insane thrill considering what they were doing. When had merriment ever accompanied this? "If you think you know how, Dewitt."

Panting, he tunneled his hand between their locked bodies, going exactly where he should. The man knew his way, a fact that aroused and infuriated her. Circling the swollen bit of skin, he whispered, "Hold on, Mountbatten."

So she did, grabbing the bedpost and pulling herself into him, where they thrust in mutual anticipation. Bumping, grinding.

Her climax was dazzling when it arrived, a shuddering storm that seized her, destroyed her. She arched her back, her cry ringing through the darkened chamber, her vision dimming. The ripples continued until she was clinging desperately to him to keep from sliding into a puddle on the floor.

"Shh, sweetness, you'll bring down the house," he said and captured her lips.

Seconds later, he trembled beneath her, his release taking hold. Lifting his hips while keeping hers in place, he thrust in long, lazy strokes that sent additional waves of pleasure careening through her.

Lastly, with an oath, he pulled free, spilling his seed between them.

What a wondrous intimacy this is when it's good, Alexandra marveled, her head dropping to Cort's shoulder in exhaustion, her breath ripping from her lungs.

When it's incredible. Devastating. Earthshattering.

How could she live without it now that she knew?

CHAPTER 6

WHERE TWO BECOME ONE, THEN TWO AGAIN

*C*ort blinked into the sunlight streaming in the window, dawn announcing itself in a burst of gilded radiance. He shoved to his elbow, a fissure of shock racing through him.

He'd slept through the night. A first since Waterloo.

He glanced to the woman curled against him, his heart giving a swift kick that denoted all kinds of horrid things. The sheet covered her, settled just above the plump curve of her magnificent breasts. A tiny tug, and he could have it around her waist. Or even better, billowing to the floor.

Where he'd then be compelled to make time disappear.

This wasn't good—and varied from his normal routine in a thousand ways. Complicating a one-night affair by staying until morning wasn't his style.

Awkward farewells were better received, and given, in the dark.

Only, he'd fallen asleep, utterly sated after the most enthralling slice of intimacy served to him in this lifetime, then roused a short time later to find Alex's mouth tracking down his chest, over his belly, headed to his awakening cock.

Any argument, weak anyway, perished on his lips, succumbing to an immediate death.

He'd let her explore for as long as he could before he'd taken over, gliding oh-so-gradually inside her, their gazes locked, an experience turning fantasy into reality. An experience he'd not shared with anyone else.

Which scared the shite out of him.

Propping his cheek on his fist, he sighed out his unease. The chamber smelled of them, each contributing to create something new, a mix he worried might never leave him. That he'd crave like an addict would opium. Trailing his fingertip across her flushed cheek, he hoped she would wake—and that she wouldn't. Because what could he say?

I'm still in love with you?

A boy's dream is now a man's?

Both sounded ridiculous. Baring his soul in this way, even if his idiocy had occurred when he was a lad, seemed the worst sort of exposure. He didn't want to be ruined by her.

He wanted to, respectfully and with consent, ruin the chits in his life—but that had never been the way with her. So, while lingering in the comfort of Viscountess Amberly's silken sheets, he acknowledged that this could be the beginning of the end.

Groaning, Cort laid back, tossing his arm over his eyes.

The lady spelled disaster for him, and she always had.

Her teasing laughter rang through the room, having the same effect as her tongue skimming along the underside of his shaft. Delight. Wicked, undeniable delight.

Lifting his arm, he peeked out to find her stunning lavender gaze fixed on him. She smiled and rolled to her side, propping her cheek on her fist as he'd done moments ago. Her hair was a catastrophe, lying in a tangle on her slim shoulders. The sheet was covering her, but not enough. Not enough at all. "From the scowl, I take it morning is not your favored time of the day."

He mirrored her posture but didn't touch her. He wasn't going there again and lose his wits. "I love mornings, in fact."

"Ah," she murmured and flashed that naughty grin, "it's *this* morning that's vexing you."

He smiled because he couldn't not. This woman turned him upside-down, much against his will. "Is this your idea of friendly discussion after the fact, Mountbatten?"

She walked her fingers across the distance, skating the rough edge of her nail over his forearm. A horsewoman's hands, his girl. His response was immediate, a fiery footrace landing in areas he'd hoped were calming. "Is it yours, DeWitt?"

He captured her hand before she could do more damage, then insanely, placed a tender kiss on the underside of her wrist. "Oh, no, I'm remarkably skilled at this sort of thing. I'm off-kilter today for some reason."

A crease split her brow as a spark of temper entered her eyes. "Yes, I've heard."

"If you'd taken me up on that kiss years ago, sad as it was, perhaps I wouldn't have felt the need to sample the market in search of consolation."

Alexandra huffed in irritation and tried to wrench free.

Cort laughed, pleased to his bones. More so when her consternation grew. *Let her stew for once.* He shrugged, this time placing a kiss on her knuckles. "I can't help what they say about me, although some of it's true. But not all. Anyway, it's Knox they're concerned about. Second sons gain little favor. Poor Damien is another step down."

"Is that why you risked your life at Waterloo? Because you felt yours held less value?"

He dropped her hand, invisible walls rising around him. He wasn't interested in discussing this. "My father never made me feel that way. My family."

"Then why? Why do it?"

With a sigh, he rolled to his back, away from her penetrating gaze. "Because I had to make my own way. I couldn't live, not in Knox's shadow, but the title's shadow. Waiting for life to find me. Rather, *I* wanted to find *it*." When he could see he hadn't shared enough, he gave her a bit more, the least he could say and not get the shakes. Or a headache that would take days to retreat. "I was a part of the King's Dragoon Guards. We had notable casualties from a surprise attack. It was challenging when I returned, pretending to be normal. But I'm better. Time is helping, as they say it does. Work is helping."

You're helping, he thought, though he couldn't admit it. Not *first,* not this time.

"The steam engine."

He turned his head, catching her gaze. "I have a talent for mechanical devices. Always have, always will. I want to know how things work, and I retain the patience to figure it out. Fortunately, mathematics is like poetry to me, my comfort with it rare. I tutored students at Cambridge or completed their work outright for a modest fee. Half the earls and viscounts in London owe me for getting them through advanced geometry. Steam travel is upon us, and I intend to make a fortune assisting England in the journey. It's not the blunt, either. I'm compelled in a way that made the decision for me."

"I've never been interested in anything but horses. Which makes me a female oddity, I realize." She pleated the sheet between her fingers, her lips pursing in thought. "You sound ambitious."

"You sound surprised." He didn't appreciate the doubt coloring her voice. Just what did this woman *think* about him? That he was a wastrel like the rest of them? He'd damned well set her straight. "What was this?" Rising to lean against the headboard, a piece he'd nearly torn off its mounting during their second session, he gestured to the erotic destruction around them. "I'd love to hear your version of the events."

Clutching silk to her bosom, she sat up, facing him. "You snuck in my home demanding one night, and I concurred. Enthusiastically. Two adults in agreement. Heavens, you made the rules. Now, here we are, dawn lighting the sky, four scores of pleasure between us. Our time at an end. If I'm not mistaken, there was an expiration date attached to this encounter."

When he continued to stare at her without comment, she punched the pillow in frustration. "You're the expert, Cort. Isn't this the way it *works?*"

"Five scores, actually, as your count totals three. Don't you remember my head situated between your thighs, where I stayed until

56

you nearly yanked my hair from my scalp? Which I adored, I might add. You taste like bloody ambrosia." Stretching his leg, he grunted, his ankle beginning to throb, as well as a stinging ache that had settled around the wound on his brow. He was botching this, he knew he was, but he couldn't stop himself from destroying the most wonderful night of his life. For protection, perhaps. Damn his fearful hide. "For the record, sweetness, I've never once made rules with you that I've been able to *keep*. Not since I was ten years old."

She squirmed, a flush crawling down her neck and beneath silk he wanted to tear apart with his bare hands. "Are we going to argue because you got what you wanted?"

"You got what you wanted, you mean."

Wrenching the sheet free and wrapping it around her body, she scrambled from the bed. "This is so like a man. Typically arrogant and short-sighted!" Striding across the chamber, she plucked her night-gown from the floor and struggled into it. Cort sighed when the crumpled satin slipped over the pale curve of her bottom, and his erection withered like a bloom torn off its stem. "The moment women seize a measure of sovereignty men have been seizing for all time, there's anarchy. Meeting as equals is promised before relations but not greatly welcomed after. If I say, *yes*, I wanted you for one night, too, but nothing more, I'm the villain."

Circling the room, she gathered his clothing, tossing his shirt and drawers at him with a delightfully feminine effort, everything landing far afield of its projected target. When she got to his cape—for some reason this garment made her angrier—she gathered it up and shook it at him with a clenched fist. "I'll take a thousand lovers if I like!" She flung his cape and watched it flutter atop the settee. "I'll proposition every handsome man in London if I elect to. Men closer to my age. Or older even!" She gestured to the wrecked sheets, the chamber, them. "Now that I *know*."

"No, you bloody won't." Cort clenched his teeth and climbed gingerly from the bed. He had a bum ankle, if she'd take a moment to recall. And he'd worked extremely hard to not let his injury interfere with her pleasure.

Lastly, she was only five years older than him, not a hundred.

"Do you think a minor infatuation when we were children means you have dominion over me? When I've finally been given a measure of freedom and found the courage to exercise it? When part of me wants to give you control. Tup you until we're both unable to walk, then do it all again." Running out of steam, she collapsed to the sofa, her chin in her hand. The movement jiggled her breasts beneath the slip of satin, which did nothing to improve his mood. "This affair business is easier there"—she pointed to the bed—"than it is outside it."

Cort stilled, one leg jammed in his trousers, his drawers tucked in a wad beneath his armpit, his shirt hanging open, the ends fluttering at his hip. *What was he doing?* He didn't want marriage. He wasn't even certain he wanted children. He'd imagined being alone, possibly, for the rest of his life until he'd stumbled upon her again. He didn't have *plans.* Knox wanted a family with such fervor Cort feared he'd marry the wrong woman to gain it.

Cort had best be happy with what had occurred this evening. His reckoning. Finding out that reality was, during the rare one-in-a-million attempt, better than any fantasy.

A headache brewing, he closed his eyes and leaned his shoulder unsteadily against the bedpost. When he opened them, Alex was staring at him with as much confusion and muted hunger as he guessed was gracing his face. "The past gives me no authority over you, sweetness. Honestly, it hampers anything we might try beyond this night because…"

"Because?"

He blew out a fierce breath and limped into his trousers, his eyes on his task, away from her. "It wasn't a minor infatuation, despite my age and immaturity. Sorrowfully, I believe I'm"—he tapped his temple—"muddled up about it still. I thought this night might overpower the dream of you when it's only made the pulse in my head stronger."

"Oh," she whispered. "*Oh.*"

"Although, I have a proposal. For both of us."

She smiled winsomely, her chin still caught in her fist. It was a flirtatious look, crisped at the edges with a hot heat that curled in his own belly. "Do you, now."

He held tight to the bedpost to keep from crossing to her. What he suspected was love was coursing through him, a blazing fire in his chest. A new set of emotions unrelated to the old, he believed, if he had a chance to untangle them. A moment to think without the scent of her clinging to his skin and taking up every inch of space in his lungs. Without the vision of her, gorgeous and rumpled from his devotion, running rampant over him.

Because if Alexandra Mountbatten came to him, ever truly *came* to him, nothing to do with the past, he needed to know it was forever.

Or she'd ruin him in a more devastating way than Waterloo had.

"Out with it, Dewitt," she murmured, courageous to the end.

"I have to be back in London in two weeks. Until then, I'm going to shut myself in my father's study and finish my designs. I'm meeting with investors in eight days." He buttoned his shirt, trying to ignore the way her gaze tracked his every move, her bottom lip caught hard between her teeth. She wanted him, if nothing else.

He was mad to deny her, to be sure, but he desired more this time, from this woman. Scratching his jaw, he blocked a laugh. What a fix he'd gotten himself in with this chit. "I promised Knox I'd attend another pointless ball. He has a prior engagement and can't. My brother has a thousand prior engagements a day, nothing new there. I'm tempted to tell everyone I'm him and see if they notice. Our old trick from Eton, which could possibly make the evening interesting."

"The Earl of Rodham's annual spring celebration. And they'll notice, Cort. I can tell you apart and have always been able to. It's ridiculous that people confuse the two of you."

Cort glanced up, something in her smile easing the emotional load on his shoulders. "You'd know me anywhere, is that it?"

Alex shrugged a slender shoulder, her teeth working her lip in a way that made him want very badly to do wicked things to her. Have her do wicked things in return, as she'd proven she could. "I've been invited as well, although I don't usually, that is, I never go to those things. Not since my first season. Ballrooms make me itchy, like I have a rash. I was only invited because I may do something scandalous the *ton* finds horrid but noteworthy. Widows are often the pinnacle of entertainment."

Cort snorted, his heart giving a quick thump. He suspected he loved this girl, to the bottom of his soul and back. "If you attend, despite the allergic reaction, find me, and I'll know. It won't be because of the lingering effects of my touch coursing through your body, my scent on your fingertips, my sweat on your skin."

"You're leaving this to me."

Easing his boot on his injured ankle, he winced. "Shall I lay my cards on the table, sweetness? It appears I must, my pride fading with the morning mist." Rising to his full height, he made sure she was looking at him when he said, "I made my decision long ago, foolish or not, and my heart hasn't forgotten. Not for one moment. Your independence may mean more to you than any man could. Maybe it should. I'm no prize, Alex. I'm a tangle, broken in part, my head full of equations. My nights often fractured by a war long over, comrades who left this world before they should've been forced to."

Searching the room, he located his coat and cape. Shrugging into them while his heart stayed across the distance. He didn't want to leave her, not even for a moment.

And that was why he must.

"Cort," she whispered, starting to rise.

"Don't. I'll never know if you come to me now, not with lust in your eyes." His gaze strayed to the bed, the tangled sheets. "I want more than being your safe bet. And maybe, just maybe, I deserve it."

Unable to restrain himself, he strode across the room, went painfully to his knee, cradled her jaw and took her lips in a consuming kiss. Her hands plunged into his hair, tugging him closer. Chest to chest, they breathed each other in.

It was magic.

Somehow, he had the power to pull away, leave her.

Knowing full well that his heart stayed behind.

CHAPTER 7

WHERE LOVE MAKES A STATEMENT

*S*he'd fallen for one of the Trio and there was no going back.

Alexandra nudged the palm frond aside and gazed across the ballroom. Nerves danced in her stomach, matching the cadence of the swirling couples gracing the floor. Her gown was from the finest modiste scant notice could buy, her coiffure so impeccably stiff her head ached. She wore her mother's sapphire earbobs and a pearl necklace in her family for centuries that was rumored to be a gift from a long-dead prince. Topping off the outfit was an empty dance card dangling from her wrist by a length of crimson velvet.

If she wished to look presentable, this was as good as it was going to get.

To appear as if she fit in with these vultures when she'd never fit in. But for him—kind, generous, tortured, exquisite, skilled-at-many-things Cortland DeWitt—she would play the game. Come to him. Admit her infatuation in front of society because her declaration was what he needed to believe he wasn't the only one in this thing.

She let the leaf glide from her fingers, where it quivered before settling back into place before her face.

Her feelings were much stronger than infatuation. She was in love with him.

It hadn't come about without intense deliberation. Nights of ceiling-staring. Scribbled lists of pros and cons about a union such as the one he'd demand of her. He wasn't a man to accept half measures.

And there was the outright spying.

People who did not want to see what was before them often didn't. Cort hadn't noticed the bedraggled domestic trailing him on his morning strolls through Hyde Park, a tattered cloak and bonnet from another era providing her adequate concealment. Nor had he seen the chit shadowing him down Bond, where he'd glanced in shop windows with a forlorn expression, not speaking when spoken to or purchasing so much as a sweet. She'd longed to halt his progress—and his angst—throw her arms around him and tell him she loved him, too.

But she'd wanted to see him again to confirm her two weeks of moping wasn't misplaced affection. Craving for his body when he was offering his soul.

It had been clear from the first second she saw him striding into the park.

She'd merely had to wait on her modiste to deliver a gown worthy of a declaration. Even if he didn't care, and she knew he didn't, she wasn't going to have him shamed for choosing to love her.

Tears pricked her eyes. She thanked the heavens he'd chosen to love her.

A footman at the top of the ballroom stairs announced Cort's name in dulcet tones and her fan tumbled to the marble floor. He was dressed in formal black except for his snowy white shirt and cravat. He'd worn his spectacles, perhaps to better see her. He leaned elegantly on a gold-tipped cane in lieu of the scuffed wooden crutch, the ideal accoutrement for the most handsome man in the room.

Alexandra watched him survey the crowd, his gaze keen, his stride pausing when he caught sight of her hiding behind a plant. His smile grew as he descended the staircase, his step sure. Certain.

A lifetime of loneliness evaporated like fog dissipated by a sharp blast of sunlight.

Flashes of remembrance battered her. His mouth at her ear, gasping his pleasure as he thrust. Riding astride his beautiful body while he whispered, "This, exactly *this*, Alex." His knuckles paling as he braced his fist on the headboard, his hips pressed to hers. All leading back to that mischievous boy, emotion she now appreciated shining in his eyes.

Halting at the bottom, his lips lifted in a half-smile.

Stepping free of her concealment, she gave a tiny shrug. *I'm here. Come and get me.*

He shrugged in return, dusting the tip of his cane through the chalk scattered across the marble floor. *I'm here. Come and get* me.

She fought a flicker of irritation and watched his smile grow. Her need for him, her *want*, was stronger than her pride, wasn't it? She couldn't forget that he'd given up part of his the morning after the most incredible night of her life. It seemed fitting, allowable, to bend slightly to his will.

She'd just have to ensure he didn't become used to it.

She desired a life with Cortland DeWitt. Her solitary childhood defeated once and for all. Mind settled, skirting the crowd, she made her way to him.

The throng parted in a bevy of fluttering fans and whispered comments. Of course, she heard them and was laughing when she reached him.

Poor man, he's fallen for the Wintry Widow.

Is that the second son or the duke?

I've heard she prefers horses to blokes.

The first in the Trio has fallen. What's to become of the other two?

"Look at that smile," he said and, shocking the crowd, drew her hand into his. "Is it for me?"

She shook her head, warmed to her toes when his fingers closed around hers. "It's for the fools I encountered on the journey."

His blinked, then he threw his head back, his amusement echoing across the ballroom.

She yanked on his hand. "Stop it, Cort. They'll never cease babbling now."

Shifting his cane under his arm, he hauled her across the floor and out the open veranda doors, uncaring who might see them. The wind ripped at her coiffure, sending strands flying. "Our marriage will set them on their bums, sweetness. This little show isn't going to make a difference. If we're patient, they'll find other victims to torture the following week. Go with it."

"Marriage—"

He had her against brick, his mouth seizing hers, before she could utter another word. His cane clattered to the flagstones as he stepped between her legs, finding her body, her heart, her *soul*, open in welcome. "You love me," he murmured against her lips.

She pushed him back enough to allow a sliver of moonlight to slip between them. Joy spread like fire through her veins. "How presumptuous."

Tipping her chin, he deepened the kiss until her knees quivered, her lungs emptying of air. "How presumptuous, *darling*."

When they'd carried the embrace as far as they could without being asked to continue after vows had been uttered, he hugged her close. His heartbeat thumped in a frantic rhythm beneath her cheek.

"I love you," she whispered into the silken threads of his waistcoat.

"I've always loved you," he returned, his lips buried in her hair. "Always. Now, gratefully, because you've finally come to your senses, I don't hate myself for it."

She lifted shining eyes to his, a tear tracking down her face. "Oh, Cort."

He dusted a kiss across her brow. "Don't. Never again with this maudlin expression. I won't stand for anything, especially the past, standing between us." Trailing his knuckle along her jaw, he captured her spent tear. "So…"

She pulled her bottom lip between her teeth, teasing him. "So…"

He tilted his head. "Is that a yes?"

"Is that a proposal?"

His chest lifted and fell on a thick exhalation. Tunneling his hand in his jacket pocket, he returned with a small velvet box. It was aged, faded with time, once a striking cherry now bleached to a pale pink. Flicking it open with trembling fingers, he swallowed, apprehension chalking grooves alongside his mouth. The ring was stunning, an emerald near the color of his eyes surrounded by a petite ring of diamonds. "It was my grandmother's. In safekeeping for the first DeWitt of this generation to pledge himself. You could have knocked Knox over with a feather when I told him I was in need of it. We had to revive Damien with smelling salts when I said it was you I'd won. The Trio is forever changed as we add another to the family. Now we're a Quad."

She reached to touch, then pulled back. She'd never been given such a lovely gift. Amberly hadn't believed in tokens of affection and her parents hadn't once thought to show her they loved her in word or offering.

Sighing softly, Cort took her hand and slid the ring on her finger. The stone glimmered in the moonlight, a promise, a future. "We'll have the jeweler make it a perfect fit. Like us."

"I'm not perfect," she whispered.

He grinned, rocking back on his heels. "Then I'm the ideal man for you, because I am."

She punched his chest. "I feel I must ask you to put this guaranteed perfection to the test."

"I love tests, sweetness." Cort grasped her hand, pulled her down the terrace stairs and into the night. "My carriage is waiting on Avery Row for just such an escape. Please make me the happiest man in England, will you? A simple 'yes, I love you and can't wait to spend my life telling you so every day' will do."

She laughed, struggling to match his eager stride. "You missed me, then."

He halted, emotion that shook her glistening in his eyes. The plink of the ancient fountain gracing the garden a melodic trill circling them. "More than life, Alex, more than life."

Laughing, they raced into the future, tears and love their guide.

EPILOGUE

WHERE PERFECTION IS SECURED

Hampstead, England 1817

*A*lexandra DeWitt didn't believe in fate.

As she stood inside the bedchamber doorway, the silence of a rainy afternoon hushed and tranquil, she gazed upon the scene before her with aching love—and felt sure she should.

The scene was enchanting, worthy of being sketched for posterity. Her husband lay sprawled on the sofa, one long leg dangling off, his arms full of their daughter, Kathleen, both of them dead asleep. The wash of emotion at the back of her throat was sudden and strong.

Her life had changed overnight with her marriage. Time spent between the DeWitt townhome in London and Hampton Court because she and Cort didn't want to be apart for even a night. Two rambunctious brothers-in-law, one a duke. Their daughter arriving thirteen months after their nuptials. They'd adopted a stray kitten they found wandering in a grimy alley behind Regent Street. Alex was working on getting Cort to agree to adopt a hound pup from a litter born in the village last week.

He'd concur eventually because he desired, more than anyone she'd ever known, to make her happy.

Her joy was boundless. She'd been given everything she'd not had. Family. A home ringing with shouts of pleasure and play. Celebrations and dinners and love. Toys scattered about, books, flowers. Nights spent in passionate splendor, mornings commencing with bliss.

Then there were the arguments—but making up was wondrous.

They'd managed to make love in every room on the estate *and* the city townhouse. Remarkably, Alex had found she had a particular fondness for amorous carriage rides and due to the amount of time they traveled, they were often in carriages.

Cort claimed to be the jolliest man in all of England.

"Are you going to wake them? We're supposed to leave in fifteen minutes for the baron's fete."

Alex glanced over her shoulder at Damien, the youngest of the Trio. He was the most mysterious DeWitt, a glow he rarely explained banked in his always-changing hazel eyes. He had secrets, more than Cort or Knox, and she often wished to pick the lock to unleash them. But he continually danced away before she could. "I vote to skip the dinner at Lord Fabien's if your niece chooses to sleep the afternoon through. She had us up all night."

"Teething," Damien murmured and popped his knuckles, an unfortunate habit, the only negative one she'd witnessed.

Alex laughed, charmed. "What do you know about teething?"

Damien shrugged. "Books."

He was the scholar of the three, rarely far from the library in any dwelling he inhabited. She worried that he'd spend his days reading about life instead of living it. The gossip rags had spilled gallons of ink over Cort and Knox but none over secretive Damien. She truly didn't know if he kept a mistress or how he chose to spend his time. And he never said a word to ease her curiosity.

"You've made him happy, Alex. After Waterloo, I worried he'd never find contentment. I understood why he went, but I feared the experience had wrecked him. That my older brother was lost to us and this shell of a man was all that was left."

Leaning against the doorjamb, love rolled over her, nearly taking her under. "He's made me the happiest of women. I didn't have a family until I was given the four of you."

Damien coughed, uncomfortable with her admission. Bumping her shoulder, he grinned. "Sisters aren't as bad as I thought they would be."

She bumped back. "Neither are brothers."

Yawning, Cort brought his hand to his lips. *Shh...* Then he slipped back to sleep, his daughter held tenderly in his arms.

Damien gave her a push that propelled her into the room. "Go be with your family," he whispered and disappeared down the corridor.

Following his advice, she did.

The End

THANK YOU!

Thank you for coming along for Cort and Alex's romantic ride!

Next in line for me in The Duchess Society series is Jasper Noble's story, *Three Sins and a Scoundrel,* releasing early 2024. I can promise second chance, second chance, second chance! My favorite trope. If you're reading the series, you know that Jasper has a lot of secrets—and a compelling heart beneath the bluster. I also have a novella in a 2023 Christmas anthology that will feature the Leighton Cluster! More to come on that.

Find an excerpt of book 1, *The Brazen Bluestocking,* at the end of this book!

Regarding the DeWitts, I'll be writing about the rest of the Trio, Damien and Knox, the Duke of Herschel, in upcoming books! Damien's story arrives in October with *The Devil of Drury Lane* and Knox's in February 2024 with *Kiss the Duke Goodbye.* (This in the Gentleman and Gloves set.)

Please sign up for my newsletter to find out about these releases and the Duchess Society fun at www.tracy-sumner.com. You'll receive a free book (the award-winning novella, *Chasing the Duke*) as my thank you. The cover is hot, hot, hot, as is the story! Also, follow me on any major retailers. It's the easiest way to get updates.

Happy reading, as always! Historical romance is the best.

xoxo

P.S. Christian Bainbridge, the watchmaker Cort mentions early in this novella, has his own love story in *Tempting the Scoundrel.* If you enjoy steamy Regency featuring class difference and love at first sight (for the hero), then this story is for you! I place a Bainbridge timepiece in the fob pocket of all my heroes!

THE BRAZEN BLUESTOCKING

THE DUCHESS SOCIETY

USA TODAY BESTSELLING AUTHOR

TRACY SUMNER

CHAPTER ONE

Limehouse Basin, London, 1822

She'd taken this assignment on a dare.

A dare to herself.

Unbridled curiosity had driven her, the kind that killed cats. When it was just another promise-of-rain winter day. Another dismal society marriage the Duchess Society was overseeing.

Another uninspiring man to investigate.

Hildegard Templeton told herself everything was normal. The warehouse had looked perfectly ordinary from the grimy cobblestones her post-chaise deposited her on. A sign swinging fearlessly in the briny gust ripping off the Thames—*Streeter, Macauley & Company* —confirming she'd arrived at the correct location. A standard, salt-wrecked dwelling set amongst tea shops and taverns, silk merchants and ropemakers. Surrounded by shouting children, overladen carts, horses, dogs, vendors selling sweetmeats and pies, and the slap of sails against ships' masts. A chaotic but essential locality, with cargo headed all over England but landing in this grubby spit of dockyard first.

When she'd stepped inside, she halted in place, realizing her blunder in assuming anything about Tobias Streeter was *normal*.

Hildy knew nothing about architecture but knew this was not the norm for a refurbished warehouse bordering the Limehouse Basin Lock. A suspect neighborhood her post-boy hadn't been pleased to drive into—or be asked to wait *in* while she conducted her business. Honestly, the building was a marvel of iron joists, girders, and cast-iron columns with ornamental heads. With a splash of elegant color—crimson and black. What she imagined a gentleman's club might look like, a refined yet dodgy sensibility she found utterly... *charming*. And entirely unnecessary for a building housing a naval merchant's headquarters.

Her exhalation left her in a vaporous cloud, and she gazed around with a feeling she didn't like as the piquant scent of a spice she identified as Asian in origin enveloped her.

A feeling she wasn't accustomed to.

Miscalculation.

As she would admit only to her business partner, Georgiana, the newly minted Duchess of Markham: *I fear I've botched the entire project.* She'd taken society's slander as truth—shipping magnate, Romani blood, profligate bounder, and the most noteworthy moniker the *ton* had ever come up with—and made up her mind about the man, concocting a wobbly plan unsupported by proper research. A proposal built on assumptions instead of *fact*. Sloppy dealings were very unlike her. Ambition to secure the agreement to advise the Earl of Hastings's five daughters as they traveled along their matrimonial journey—the eldest currently set on marrying the profligate bounder —had risen above common sense.

Hildy took a breath scented with exotic spice and tidal mud and stepped deeper into the warehouse, locking her apprehension out of sight. She wasn't going to back down now, not when she had *five* delightful but wholly unsupervised women who would make terrific disasters of their marriages without the Duchess Society to guide them.

Marriages much like her parents' were an aberration staining her memories until she wanted none of the institution. They needed her, these girls, and she needed *them*. To prove her life wasn't a tale as ordinary as the building she'd expected to find herself in this morning —society outcast, bluestocking. Spinster. Not that it mattered what they thought of her; she'd rejected the expectations the *ton* had placed on her from the first moment.

"Looking for Streeter, are ya?"

Hildy turned in a swirl of flounces and worsted wool she wished she'd rejected for this visit when a simple day dress would have sufficed. Perhaps one borrowed from her maid.

The man who'd stumbled upon her lingering in the entrance to the warehouse was tall enough to have her arching her neck to view him from beneath her bonnet's lime silk brim. And built like one of those ships moored at the wharf outside. "Tobias Streeter, yes."

The brute gave the tawny hair lying across his brow a swipe, removed the cheroot from his lips, and extinguished it beneath the toe of his muddy boot in a gesture she didn't think the architect of this impressive building would appreciate. "He expecting ya?"

They make them rude in the East End, Hildy decided with a sigh. "Possibly." If he'd been alerted by his future father-in-law, *yes*.

"Who's calling?" he asked gruffly, digging in his pocket and coming up with another cheroot, even as the bitter aroma from the first still enveloped them. "Apologies for asking, but we don't get many of your kind round here. Some kinds"—he chuckled at his joke and swiped the tapered end of the cheroot across his bottom lip—"just not *your* kind."

Hildy shifted the folio she clutched from one gloved hand to the other. Her palms had started to perspire beneath kid leather. This man was playing with her, and she didn't like participating in games she wasn't sure she could win. "Lady Hildegard Templeton," she supplied, using the honorific when she rarely did. "Of the Duchess Society."

The impolite brute arrested his effort to remove a tinderbox from his tattered coat pocket. "The Mad Matchmaker," he whispered, his cheroot hitting the glossy planks beneath their feet. Horrified, he backed up a step as if she had a contagious disease.

A rush of blood flooded her. *Temper*, she warned herself. *Not here.* The blush lit her cheeks, and she cursed the man standing stunned before her for causing it. "That ridiculous sobriquet is not something I respond—"

"Sobriquet," a voice full of laughter and arrogance intoned from behind her. "Go back to unloading the shipment from Spain, Alton. I have this."

When she turned to face the man she assumed was Tobias Streeter, she wanted to be in control because that was how this day was going to go. Confident. Poised. Looking like a businesswoman, not a lady. Not a *matchmaker*—which she *wasn't*. She longed to tell him what she thought of the rude entry to his establishment when he hadn't known she was coming.

Instead, she felt flushed and damp, unprepared based on a split-second judgment of the glorious building she stood in. Adding to that, the niggling sense that she'd made a colossal error in calculating her opponent.

And then Hildy merely felt *thunderstruck*.

Because, as he stepped out of the shadows and into the glow cast from the garnet sconce at his side, she realized with a heavy heart that Tobias Streeter, the Rogue King of Limehouse Basin, was the most attractive man she'd ever seen.

Which wasn't an asset. She was considered attractive as well—she surmised with a complete and utter lack of vanity—and she'd only found it to be a *trap*.

"I wondered if you'd actually venture into the abyss, luv," he said idly, tugging a kerchief from his back pocket and across his sweaty brow.

He had a streak of graphite on his left cheek, and his hands were a further mess. Additionally, he'd made no effort to contain the twisted collar of his shirt. The top two bone buttons were undone, and the flash of olive skin drew her gaze when she wished it wouldn't. No coat, no waistcoat. He was unprepared for visitors.

However, if she were being fair, she'd given him no notice he was to have one.

"Those feral phaeton rides through Hyde Park I read about in the *Gazette* must be true. They say you're a daredevil at heart, Templeton, a feminine trait the *ton* despises, am I right? Gossip that I'd lay odds you don't welcome any more than that charming nickname your poisonous brethren saddled you with." He tucked the length of stained cloth in his waistband to crudely dangle, drawing her eye to his trim waist. "They can't understand anyone of means who doesn't simply sit back and enjoy it."

"I'm, well..." Hildy fumbled, then wished she'd waited another moment to gather her thoughts. "I'm here on business. As you know. Or guessed."

His gaze dropped to the folio in her hand, his lips quirking sourly. "My sordid past is bundled up in that tidy file, I'm guessing."

No, actually, she wanted to admit but thankfully didn't. *I've gone into this all wrong.*

She ran through the facts detailed on the sheet in her wafer-thin folio that were not facts at all. Royal Navy hero of some sort, a conflict in India he didn't discuss publicly. Powerful friends in the East India Company, hence his move into trade upon his return to England. Ruthless, having built his empire one brick at a time. Father rumored to be titled, mother of Romani stock, at least a smidgen, which was all it took to be completely ostracized.

Insanely handsome had never factored into her research.

And she'd assumed this would be an uncomplicated assignment.

"Tobias Streeter," he murmured, halting before her. Almost as tall as his brutish gatekeeper, Hildy kept her head tilted to capture his gaze. Which she was going to capture. And *hold*. Hazy light from a careless sun washed over him from windows set at all angles, allowing her to peruse at her leisure.

She didn't fool herself; it was an opportunity he *allowed*.

Skin the color of lightly brewed tea. Eyes the shade of a juicy green apple you shined against your sleeve and then couldn't help but take a quick bite of—the glow from the sconce turning them a deep emerald while she stared. Highlighted by a set of thick lashes any woman would be jealous of. Jaw hard, lips full, breath scented with mint and tea. Not brandy or scotch, another misstep had she presumed it.

When, of course, she'd presumed it.

As he patiently accepted her appraisal, his hand rose, and his index finger, just the calloused tip, trailed her cheek to tuck a stray strand behind her ear.

The hands of a man who worked with them.

Played with them.

She shivered, a shallow exhalation she couldn't contain rushing forth in a steamy puff. Parts of the ground story were open from quay to yard for transit handling, and glacial gusts were whistling through like a train on tracks.

"Alton," he instructed without glancing away from her, though he dropped his hand to his side. "Close the doors at the back, will you? And bring tea to my office."

"Tea," Alton echoed. "*Tea?*"

Streeter's breath fanned her face, warming her to her toes. "Isn't that what ladies drink over business dealings? If ladies even *do* business. Perhaps it's what they drink over spirited discussions about watercolors or their latest gown."

She gripped the folio until her knuckles ached, feeling like a ball of yarn being tossed between two cats. "Make no special accommodations. I'll have whatever it is you guzzle during business dealings, Mr. Streeter."

He laughed, then caught himself with the slightest downward tilt of his lips. She'd surprised them both somehow. It was the first chess move she'd won in this match. "We guzzle malt whiskey then," he murmured and turned, seeming to expect her to follow.

She recorded details as she shadowed him across the vast space crowded with shipping crates and assorted stacks of rope and tools, to a small room at the back overlooking the pier. His shirt was untucked on one side, the kerchief he'd wiped his face with slapping his thigh. His clothing was finely made but not skillfully enough to hide a muscular build most men used built-in padding to establish. Dark hair, *no*, more than dark. Black as tar, curling over his rumpled shirt collar and around his ears. So pitch dark, she imagined she could see cobalt streaks in it, like a flame gone mad.

Hair that called a woman's fingers to tangle in it, no matter the woman.

The gods had allotted this conceited beast an inequitable share of beauty, that was certain. And for the first time in her *life*, Hildy was caught up in an attraction.

His office was another unsurprising surprise.

A roaring fire in the hearth chasing away the chill. A Carlton House desk flanked by two armchairs roomy enough to fit Streeter or his man of business, Alton. A Hepplewhite desk, or a passable imitation. A colorful Aubusson covering the floor, nothing threadbare and old because it had lost its value. Her heart skipped as she stepped inside the space, confirmation that she'd indeed misjudged. Shelf upon shelf of leather-bound books bracketed the walls. Walking to a row, she checked the spines with a searching review. Cracked but good, each and every one of them. Architecture, commerce, mathematics, chemistry. Nothing entertaining, nothing playful. The library of a man with a mind.

While Streeter moved to a sideboard that had likely come from the king's castoffs, and poured them a drink from a bottle whose label she didn't recognize, she circled the room, inspecting.

Holding both glasses in one hand, he situated himself not at his desk but on the edge of an overturned crate beside it, his long legs stretched before him. Sipping from his while holding hers, his steely gaze tracked her. Fortunately, she realized from the travel-weary Wellington he tapped lightly on the carpet, her examination of his private space was making him uneasy. With an aggrieved grunt, he yanked the kerchief from his waistband and tossed it needlessly to the floor.

Finally, she sighed in relief, a *weakness*. If he didn't like to be studied, he must have *something* to hide. She'd been hired, in part, to find out what.

"This isn't one of your frivolous races through the park." He leaned to place her glass on the corner of his desk. Hers to take, or not, when she passed. The only charitable thing he'd done was pour it for her. "Right now, I have two men guarding your traveling chariot parked outside, lest someone rob you blind. The thing is as yellow as a ripe banana, which catches the eye. They'll slice the velvet from the squabs and resell it two blocks over for fast profit. Your post-boy looked ready to expire when we got to him. Guessing he's never had to sit on his duff while waiting for his mistress to complete business in the East End. A slightly larger *man* might better fit the bill next time."

Post-boys were all she could afford.

Hildy released the satin chin strap and slid her bonnet from her head. Her coiffure, unsteady on a good day as her maid's vision was dreadful, collapsed with the removal, and a wave of hair just a shade darker than the sun fell past her shoulders. Streeter blinked, his fingers tightening around his glass. She noticed the insignificant gesture while wondering if the fevered awareness filling the air was only in *her* mind.

Halting by his desk, she reached for her drink with a nod in his direction. The scent of soap and spice drifted to her, his unique mix. "This warehouse, it's quite unusual. Magnificent, actually. I've never seen the like."

"I'll be sure to tell the architect the daughter of an earl approves." His gaze cool, giving away absolutely nothing, he dug a bamboo toothpick from his trouser pocket and jammed it between his teeth, working it from side to side between a pair of very firm lips. At her raised brow, he shrugged. "Stopped smoking. It's enough to breathe London's coal-laden air without asking for more trouble."

Hildy dropped the folio, which held little of value aside from her employment contract with the Earl of Hastings, in the armchair and lifted the glass to her lips. The whiskey was smooth, smoky—*good*. "This is excellent," she mused, licking her lips and watching Streeter's hand again tense around his tumbler.

"Thank you. It's my own formula," he said after a charged silence, a dent appearing next to his mouth. Not so much a dimple. Two of which she had herself, a feature people had commented on her entire life.

His was more of an elevated smirk.

"Yours?" Continuing her journey around the room, Hildy paused by a framed blueprint of this warehouse. Beside it was another detailed sketch, a building she didn't recognize. Architectural schematics drawn by someone very talented. She couldn't miss the initials, *TS*, in the lower right corner.

Frowning, she tilted her glass, staring into it as if the amber liquor would provide answers to an increasingly enigmatic puzzle. Aside from disappointing her family and society, she'd never done anything remarkable. *Been* anything remarkable.

When faced with remarkability, she wasn't sure she trusted it.

Streeter stacked his boots one atop the other, the crate creaking beneath him. "A business venture, a distillery going south financially that I found myself uncommonly intrigued by, once I handed over an astounding amount of blunt to keep it afloat *and* demanded I be invited into the process. Usually, I invest, then step away if the enterprise is well-managed, which it often isn't, but this..." Bringing the glass to his lips, he drank around the toothpick. Quite a feat. She couldn't look away from the show of masculine bravado if she'd been ordered to at the end of a pistol. "It's straightforward chemistry, the brewing of malt. But, lud, what a challenge, seeking perfection."

Finessing his glass into an empty spot next to him on the crate, he wiggled the toothpick from his lips and pointed it at her. A crude signal that he was ready to begin negotiations. "Isn't seeking perfection your business too, luv? The *ideal* bloke, without shortcomings. I've yet to see such a man, but the Mad Matchmaker is fabled to work miracles, so maybe there's a chance for me."

Seating herself in the chair absent her paperwork, Hildy set her glass on the desk and worked her gloves free, one deliberate finger at a time. If he believed he could chase her away with his bullying attitude, he hadn't done suitable research into his opponent's background. Last year, the Duchess Society had completed an assignment, confidential in nature but rumored nonetheless, for the royal family.

Madness, power, fantastic wealth, love gained, love lost. This handsome scoundrel and his trifling reach for society's acceptance, she could handle.

Although she realized she was silently reminding herself of the fact, not stating it outright.

"Nothing to do with perfection and rarely anything to do with love, Mr. Streeter. The betrothals I support are, like the marriage you're proposing with Lady Matilda Delacour-Baynham, a business agreement. Unless I'm mistaken from the discussions I've had with her and her father, the Earl of Hastings."

He twirled the toothpick between his fingers like a magician. "You have it dead on. Holy hell, I'm not looking for love. Don't fill the chit's head with that rubbish. The words mean nothing to me. They never have. Society only sells the idea to make the necessity of unions such as these more acceptable."

Well, *that* sounded personal. "Lady Matilda—"

"Mattie wants freedom. If you know her, she's told you what she's interested in. The only thing. Medicine." He laughed and sent the toothpick spinning. "An earl's daughter, can you conjure it? When no female can be a physician and certainly not a legitimate lady. To use one of your brethren's expressions, it's beyond the pale."

He winked at her, *winked*, and she was reasonably certain he didn't mean it playfully.

"I have funds, more than she can spend in a lifetime. More than I can. She wants to use a trifling bit to rescue her father, a man currently drowning, and I do mean drowning, in debt? Fine. Finance her hobby of practicing medicine? Also fine. Or her *dream*, if you're the visionary sort. Let her safely prowl these corridors and others on the rookery trail, delivering babes, bandaging wounds, swabbing fevered brows. They have no one else, the desperate souls I live amongst. She'll be an angel in their midst. And me, the one controlling the deliverance. Deliverance for *her* from your upmarket bunch. Who, other than finding ways to creatively lose capital, do nothing but sit around on their arses making up nicknames for those who *prosper*."

"What's in it for you?" Hildy whispered, not sure she knew. Was

Tobias Streeter, rookery bandit, shipping titan, this eager to marry into a crowd that indeed sat on their toffs all day dreaming up pointless monikers? When she'd been trying to escape them her entire *life*?

He jabbed the toothpick in her direction, his smile positively savage. "Don't worry about what I need. I don't make deals where I don't profit, luv."

A caged tiger set loose on society. That's what he was. Half of London was secretly fawning over him while refusing him admittance to their sacred drawing rooms.

Not so fussy about admittance to their beds, she'd bet.

He slipped the toothpick home between his stubbornly compressed lips. "Templeton, you of all people should understand her predicament, being somewhat peculiar yourself. Boxed in by society's expectations, unless I'm missing my guess, which I usually don't. I understand, do you see? It's why the girl trusts me. Why, maybe, I trust *her*.

"I know what it's like to be found lacking for elements beyond your control. Where you were born, the color of your skin. Being delivered on the wrong side of some addled viscount's blanket. Think nothing of intelligence or courage, wit or ingenuity, *talent*, only the blue blood, or lack of it, running beneath that no one sees unless you slice them open."

Hildy smoothed her hand down her bodice and laid her gloves in a neat tangle on her knee, Streeter chasing every move with his intense, sea-green gaze. That blasted blue blood he spoke of kept her tangled in a web, day in and day out. He didn't need to enlighten her. Resignedly, she nodded to the folio lying like a spent weapon between them.

"Let's discuss specifics, shall we? Hastings wants you to court his daughter properly. Even if Lady... um, Mattie doesn't require it, *he* does. Flowers, gifts, trinkets. Courtship rituals. The servants gossip, and everyone in London then knows what's what, so this is an essential, seemingly trivial part of the process. I'll assist with the selection. He'd also like certain businesses you're involved with downplayed, so to speak. The unsavory enterprises. At least until the first babe is born. Rogue King of Limehouse Basin isn't exactly what he desired for his darling girl. But you, obviously, got to her first."

"At least I'm not an ivory-turner," he whispered beneath his breath.

She tilted her head in confusion.

"Her father cheats at dice, my naïve hoyden. I do many cursed things, but cheating is not one. Every gaming hell in town is after him." Streeter growled and, snatching up his glass, polished off the contents. Lord, she wished he'd button his collar. The view was becoming a distraction. "There's more to this agreement. I can see from the brutal twist of those comely lips of yours. More edges to be smoothed away like sandpaper to rough timber. Go on, spit it out. I can take a ruthless assessment."

Hildy controlled, through diligence born of her own beatdowns, the urge to raise her hand to cover her lips. *Comely* ones that had begun to sting pleasantly at his backhanded compliment. "Aside from your agreement that my solicitors—in addition to yours and the earl's —will review all contracts to ensure fairness for both parties, there is the matter of Miss Henson."

He whispered a curse against crystal and was unapologetic when his narrowed gaze met hers. He lowered his glass until it rested on his flat belly. "So, I'm to play the holy man until the ceremony?" Then he muttered something she didn't catch. Or didn't want to. *For a wife who prefers women.*

Hildy made a mental note to investigate that disastrous possibility, although it made no difference. Lady Matilda—Mattie—had to get married to someone. A *male* someone. Why not this beautiful devil who seemed to actually *like* her? Heavens, Hildy thought in despair. The Duchess Society couldn't weather the storm should a scandal of that magnitude come to light. It was illegal, which was absurd, of course, but that was the case. There were whisperings of such goings-on, relationships on the sly.

Rumors with the power to destroy one's *life*.

It was decided at that moment, with dust motes swirling through fading wintry sunlight, in a startlingly elegant office in the middle of a slum. This marriage, between a lady who wanted to be a doctor but couldn't and a tenacious blackguard who wanted high society tucked neatly in his pocket, had to happen. Or Hildy and her enterprise to save the women of London from gross matrimonial injustice was *finished*.

Too, she would go belly up without funds coming in to pay the bills—and coming in *soon*.

Streeter rocked forward, his Wellingtons dusting the floor, upsetting the shipping crate until she feared it would collapse beneath him. "I return the question because it's a valuable one. Besides a hefty fee that Hastings can't afford and will eventually derive from other sources, namely the source sharing this stale malt air with you, what's in it for you? Dealing with me isn't going to be easy. Ask my partners, should you be able to locate them. Mattie isn't much better from what I know of her. Her spirit is part of the reason I believed she'd be the right woman for the job."

Hildy chewed on her bottom lip, an abominable habit, then glanced up to find Streeter's gaze had gone vacant around the edges. The way a man's does when he's *thinking* about things. She wasn't, saints above, imagining the thread of attraction strung between them like ship's netting. He felt it, too. "I'll be candid."

"Please do," he whispered, bringing himself back from his musing, his cheeks slightly tinged. His breathing maybe, *maybe*, churning faster.

"When I arrived, I would've said I was doing it to secure future business with the Earl of Hastings. He has five daughters, as you know, and no wife to guide them. A line of inept governesses, another quitting every week it seems. My proposal?

"I guide him to appropriate men for the remaining four since Mattie has you on the hook. *Decent* men my people have investigated thoroughly. Then assist with the negotiations, so his daughters are protected, pay my coal bill, and we're both happy." Hildy ran her finger over a nap in the chair's velvet, her gaze dropping to record her progress. "Frankly, I need the money as I wasn't left a large inheritance, more a burden. An ever-maturing residence and staff and no funds allocated for preservation.

"And I'm not planning to marry myself, so survival falls directly to me. Likewise, I do this to benefit the young women I work with, if you must know, not simply as a business venture. You have no idea how lacking they are simply from being isolated from any discussions outside the appropriate tea to serve. They're forced to sign contracts they can't even begin to understand—*lifelong*, binding contracts—with no assistance."

The toothpick bounced in Streeter's mouth as he bit down on it. "What's changed?"

Digging her fingertips into the chair's cushion, she decided to tell him. "I'm *bored* with earls and viscounts in fretful need of an heir to carry on a line that should cease production. In need of capital to salvage a crumbling empire. A rumored Romani bastard who's hiding what he really wants, and I'm the person hired to find out what?" She snapped her fingers, a weight lifting as she spoke the truth. "Now, there's a challenge."

For a breathless second, Streeter's face erased of expression. Like a fist swept across a mirror's vapor. She'd stunned him—and her pulse soared. Foolishly, categorically. Then a broad smile, a *sincere* smile, sent the dent in his cheek pinging. His teeth flashed in wonderfully startling contrast to his olive skin. "Well, damn, I can be surprised." He saluted her with the glass he'd picked up only to find it empty. "A worthy opponent steps out of the mist."

"I'm not an opponent," she murmured, knowing she was.

With a sigh of regret, perhaps because she'd gone back to fibbing, he braced his hand on his thigh and rose to his feet. She watched him cross the room because she couldn't help herself. Tall, broad yet lean, an awe-inspiring physique even in mussed clothing. He moved with an innate grace even a duke wouldn't necessarily have possessed. Natural and unassuming. The stuff one was born with—or without. Elegance that simply was.

He stopped before another of the schematic drawings, an imposing brick structure laid out with mathematical precision she suspected existed only in the sketch. "What if I say no to working with you? Refuse your kind service. Toss it back to Hastings like a flaming ember, pitting his desperation against my ambition."

Hildy understood after a moment's panic that this was part of the negotiation. That the correct response, or non-response, was vital. Retrieving her glass, she took a generous pull, smooth liquor chasing away the chill. "Is it any different than working with your"—she gestured over her shoulder to the warehouse—"bountiful trading partners? We'll be in business together. End of story."

He paused, studying her in a way few men had dared to even while telling her how beautiful she was. Men she'd never wanted to undress her with their eyes, as the saying went. A phrase that until this second had held no meaning.

A peculiar tension, the awareness from earlier, roared between them as if Alton had reopened the doors and let the Thames rush in. As if Tobias Streeter had laid his hands on her. An experience she had no familiarity with which to visualize.

"End of story," he murmured joylessly and turned back to his sketch.

She deposited her folio on his desk, the thump ringing through the room. Outside, a dockworker's shout and the rub and bump of a ship sliding into harbor pierced the hush. He was equally damaged, she could see. And very good at hiding it. They were alike in this regard, a mysterious element only another wounded animal would recognize.

Making the call on instinct alone, Hildy nonetheless made it.

Tobias Streeter wasn't a fiend. He wasn't an abuser like her father.

He was just a man.

A man she was willing to polish until he shone like the crown jewels. "There will be events. Part of your engagement and introduction to the *ton*, as it were. You'll likely need some instruction."

He tapped the sketch three times before shifting to lean his shoulder against the wall in a negligent slump she no longer counted as factual. "I clean up well. Never fear," he said, his voice laced with scorn. Who it was directed at, she wasn't sure. "I'll review the contract in that tasteful folio of yours this evening, then we'll discuss the details tomorrow afternoon. I'll send a carriage with a coachman ready to protect you should the need arise, not those lads just out of the schoolroom you have manning your conveyance."

Glancing to a clock on the mantel that had been cautiously ticking off time, his smile thinned, frigid enough to freeze water. "I'm sorry to rush you out, but I have a meeting in ten minutes that will, if successful, net me close to a thousand pounds. My men will escort you home. Your chariot can follow along for fun." His jaw tensed when she started to argue, and he pushed off the wall with a growl. "Not on my watch, Templeton. Not in my township. Don't even *begin*."

However, stubborn chit that she was, she did begin, opening her mouth to tell him who was managing this campaign to show London how bloody wonderful a husband he would be.

"Tea and some of them lemony biscuits from the baker on the corner, coming right up," Alton proclaimed, stumbling into the room, a silver teapot she wondered where in heaven's name he'd located clutched in a meaty fist and two mismatched china cups balanced in the other. Halting, he took one look at his employer's thunderous expression, slapped the cups on the first available surface, and hustled Hildy from the office.

The teapot was still in his hand as Streeter's coach rolled down the congested lane with her an unwilling captive inside. She suppressed a clumsy laugh to see a coat of arms, painted over but visible, on the carriage's door.

Another aristocrat who'd lost his fortune to the Rogue King.

Hildy collapsed against the plush squabs of the finest transport she'd ever ridden in, realizing she hadn't asked Tobias Streeter how he planned to profit from a marriage he didn't want.

ABOUT TRACY

USA Today bestselling author Tracy's story telling career began when she picked up a copy of LaVyrle Spencer's Vows on a college beach trip. A journalism degree and a thousand romance novels later, she decided to try her hand at writing a southern version of the perfect love story. With a great deal of luck and more than a bit of perseverance, she sold her first novel to Kensington Publishing.

When not writing sensual stories featuring complex characters and lush settings, Tracy can be found reading romance, snowboarding, watching college football and figuring out how she can get to 100 countries before she kicks. She lives in the south, but after spending a few years in NYC, considers herself a New Yorker at heart.

Tracy has been awarded the National Reader's Choice, the Write Touch and the Beacon—with finalist nominations in the HOLT Medallion, Heart of Romance, Rising Stars and Reader's Choice. Her books have been translated into German, Dutch, Portuguese and Spanish. She loves hearing from readers about why she tends to pit her hero and heroine against each other from the very first page or that great romance she simply must order.

Connect with Tracy on http://www.tracy-sumner.com